Carry the Day

By: Yashica M. Smith

Acknowledgements

It's funny how God works. I had chosen the cover for this book long before I had actually done any research. So I had no clue whether or not the Sunflower image pictured even related to the story. I simply picked it because I thought it looked nice.

Once I did my research, I was amazed to learn that the Sunflower is considered a symbolism for faith and optimism. It's said that the flower tends to grow towards the sunlight because it hopes for better days. Not only did I find this information amazing but naturally all I could do was smile. Especially, since this journey has been long.

To my Lord & Savior, you are amazing beyond anything I could ever imagine and you deserve a Hallelujah kind of praise. I am not worthy of the favor you have bestowed upon me.

To all of my family and friends, you guys just don't know how much it means to have people in your life who are willing to fill in the gaps for you. You all kept me inspired, motivated and I cannot say THANK YOU enough! I am beyond blessed to have such a beautiful host of family & friends!

I want to give a special thank you to Brandi Graves, Charisse Everett, Kimberly Riggins, Andrea Walker and Tia White for all your help.
I dedicate this book to my daughter Autumn, my niece and nephew Chloe' and Tristan.

Chapter 1

Somehow, by chance or fate I was chosen to live a life full of uncontrollable circumstances. In many cases I made decisions that put my journey into someone else's hands. Some were bad, some were great, but either way here I am to share my journey.

Now, where do I start?

My name is Phadila Lombardijones. I'm from Bed-Stuy, Brooklyn. I grew up in the projects; does it really matter which one? We're all in the same circumstances. I lived not too far from Brown's laundromat, known to many as the spot for gossip around the neighborhood. Every other Saturday morning my mom, my older sister, Phalana, and I would go there to wash our clothes. I really hated washing clothes, but I loved spending the time with my mom and sister was our strange little way of bonding.

At Brown's we got to see everyone, and we never missed a beat. You never knew what would take place, who would be there, or what new gossip you'd hear maybe even about yourself. I can remember the day my mom found out that my oldest brother, Ohaji, was having sex. I was about eight years old, and Ohaji was fourteen. Mrs. Nolden, known as the community complainer confronted my mom about her daughter. No one liked her because she bitched about everything, especially things that didn't have anything to do with her.

I can remember it like it was yesterday, Mrs. Nolden walked into the laundromat that day wearing her usual black stretch pants, long T-shirt, and hot pink fluffy slippers. She came in heavy-footed, with her hands on her hip storming right over to my momma.

"Georgia Lombardijones, I knew I'd see you here. I have a bone to pick with you."

My mother looked around as if Mrs. Nolden weren't talking to her and responded, "Come again?"

My sister giggled. She was always amused by my mom's random phrases.

"Yes, you!" Mrs. Nolden searched the room as well, turning back to my mom. "No need to look around. I'm going to say this one time and one time only. You keep your nappy headed thug away from my daughter before I shoot his skinny tail myself."

My momma rose up out of her seat calmly. Everyone in the laundromat stood quiet as mice excited to see the show.

"Excuse me?" she asked. "Maybe I missed something."

Mrs. Nolden moved in a little closer to my mom so she could hear a little better, "I take it you missed what I said because either you're slow or you have no control over your children."

My mom stood to her feet proudly making it clear she was not backing down.

"I caught your son in my house with my daughter having sex," Mrs. Nolden went on. "She told me they've been having sex for a month now, and I'm telling you to keep him away from her. If I find out he's even been breathing on my daughter, I'll shoot him down." Mrs. Nolden looked very sure she got her point across to my mom, who still hadn't budged one bit besides a raised eyebrow.

"Mrs. Nolden, one thing I've never had a problem with is teaching my children. I will have a talk with my son, and I will tell *you* this: don't you ever say you're going to bring any kind of harm to my children, because I personally will wipe your miserable ass off the earth."

My sister and I giggled.

My mom continued, "While you're so worried about my son clearly you don't know your daughter because you wasn't worried about her with Sheryl's son last week or Cynthia's son Chris the week before. Your daughter is loose. Everyone seems to know it but you. I'll have a word with my son, and you may want to have a word and with your daughter. Until then don't ever address me like I won't whoop your ass."

My mom gave Mrs. Nolden her famous head nod and proceeded to separate her clothes.

Personally, I was hoping Mom would hit her at least twice, but she didn't. I guess there was no need because Mrs. Nolden walked out of the Laundromat ashamed. I guess my mom's words were worse than getting her butt whooped. I'm pretty sure my mom could have whooped her up something nice.

My mom was so mad the rest of the time it took us to finish washing and drying our clothes. Neither my sister nor I said a word. I could see it all in Mom's face: she was planning what she'd say to my brother once we got back home. When we left the laundromat, Phalana and I made sure we walked a few steps behind her because we didn't want to upset her anymore than she already was. As we hit the corner, we saw my brothers and their friends sitting on the steps of our building. A couple of them jumped up offering to help with the basket of clothes, but Mom had something else in mind.

"Ohaji, come in the house for a second."

Yes, ma'am," my brother replied, a bit confused. He looked to me and Phalana for a heads-up.

"Ohhh, you're in trouble," I said, giggling and closing the door behind us all.

"Girls," Mom said, "fold the clothes and put them away for me. Ohaji, come in the kitchen."

My sister and I pulled the basket into the living room so we could hear their conversation. But we couldn't hear a word. We did hear our Dad say, "I'm going to have to talk to you about it later today, after I rest." But that was it. I was kind of upset; he didn't get into any real trouble. Maybe it was a kid like thing to see your siblings get into trouble.

Though he didn't seem to be in big trouble my mom stormed out the kitchen yelling, "I don't want any babies in my house. If any one of you comes in here with one, you better be planning to move out, period! Shit, I can barely feed my own." She rambled on and on, as parents do about everything.

Chapter 2

In our project building, there was only one way in and one way out. We lived on the second floor, crammed into a two-bedroom apartment. The living room and kitchen were the biggest rooms. My parents bought a divider to put in one bedroom to separate the girls from the boys. It was the best they could do. We didn't have much money, and my parents were too proud to take any handouts. We were extremely rich in love, and in their eyes that was enough.

My parents made sure we had just enough to not focus so much on what we didn't have. They were always a team. We couldn't ever put one against the other. They have always been absolutely in love with each other and inseparable. I hardly ever heard them complain. I did hear them argue once or twice, but never in front of us. Well, except the time my dad broke the news to us that Santa Claus didn't really exist. My mom was furious. Guess she thought we should've believed in Santa forever. Dad was always a realist and Mom was the voice of possibilities. They balanced one another.

I talk about my parents a lot because they mean the world to me. They've been together for almost thirty-five years. They met in Brooklyn when my mom was fifteen and my dad was sixteen. My dad was hanging out on Malcolm X Boulevard, outside a barbershop one day when my Mom walked past. He followed her down the street until she gave him her phone number. From there on they started dating and fell madly in love.

Once my mom turned eighteen, they got married without telling their families. They didn't think their parents would approve of such a young union. But their love for each other was real, and nothing could come between them. They had their wedding at the courthouse and started their own legacy by putting their last names together to form Lombardijones. My grandparents eventually found out about the wedding, and they weren't as mad as my parents had thought they'd be. They were just upset that they didn't have the chance to throw a big celebration.

I admire everything about my parent's marriage. They've always kept it fresh. They would buy each other little gifts unexpectedly, have dinner dates, things like that. To this day they're my image of perfection.

My father is a Lombardi; he's both Italian and Dominican. My grandparents left Brazil for America when my dad, who's the youngest of five boys was eight.

My mother is Chinese-Trinidadian and African American. After my grandfather was murdered for his fruit stand in Trinidad, my grandmother moved all her children to America for a better life.

My parents have four children; two girls and two boys. My Brother Ohaji who is the oldest, my parents had him two years after they got married. He's the level-headed one, very private, smart, and ambitious. He and I are extremely close. We tell each other everything.

The second oldest is my sister Phalana. She's girly, loud, and funny. Think pink and you've hit her personality on the head. She and I are close as well, mostly when it comes to teaching each other about men.

The third oldest is Christian. He's the rebel. He loves sports and tattoos, and he's free-spirited. My two brothers are like night and day. The only passion they've ever shared is sports. Ohaji played football all his life, and Christian played soccer and baseball. If they weren't brothers they never would have crossed each other's path.

Last but not least is me Phadila. I'm outgoing but laid back, a tomboy but a fashion queen. You'll learn about me as we go on. My siblings and I are all very different, but we're close, and family means everything to us. We have one common personality trait: we're all very outspoken. We don't bite our tongues for anyone. It's something our parents firmly believe in.

My mother was an elementary school teacher and my father was a night shift butcher. He always went to work after dinner and came home in the morning, when we were getting ready for school. I sometimes felt like he wasn't there for me, but I understood why. He loved his job though it didn't pay much.

I hated the place where my dad worked. He took me to visit a few times, and it always had the worst smell. Something about seeing raw meat just hanging around yuck! That place could be the reason why I hate meat to this day, or maybe it's because we ate so much of it while I was growing up. Dad had grown accustomed to it, it didn't bother him. It also didn't bother my mom because she was just happy he had a paying job.

Every morning my mom woke us up bright and early for school. First she would make breakfast, then get us girls up because we needed more time. Usually my dad walked in the front door just as we were leaving. Every time he would head right to bed.

School was a ten minute walk, though in the winter, when there was snow everywhere, it seemed to take hours. On Fridays we caught the bus a splurge from my mom. Once we got to school we always ate breakfast again. Even though both my parents worked, there wasn't much money to go around after the bills and rent were paid. Usually what she made us in the morning wasn't enough. Which means we got free lunch and we made sure we didn't miss a meal.

Unlike a lot of my friends whose parents got food stamps, mine had too much pride to even apply. I would have signed up with no problem or shame. But my parents believed that since it was their choice to have kids, it was their responsibility to take care of us without handouts. That was one of their many theories I never understood. We needed all the help we could get. And if we I tried to say something about it, that was when their love for having outspoken kids quickly ceased. Then it we were being disrespectful to speak up. Personally, I thought their decision was selfish, but I have to admit it brought us closer as a family having to go without and constantly have to share everything.

* * *

My siblings and I are each two years apart and as kids we shared the same best friends. Many of who were the kids of my mom's best friend, Ms. Gloria. She was one of the first people Mom had met when her family came to America. They gone to school together and lived in the same neighborhood all their lives. They've been best friends since they were twelve years old.

I'm not sure if my mom and Ms. Gloria planned to have their kids around the same time, but that was what happened. Ms. Gloria had five kids, three girls and two boys. Ms. Gloria, was also a teachers. None of her kids ever missed a day even when they were sick. They never complained. I guess they loved school. I was there for meals, of course; but it was nice to be in an environment where I didn't have to worry about what was going on at home for a few hours a day. I was a kid, but I was very observant and paid attention to the littlest things. I often saw my parents talking at the kitchen table about bills not adding up and figuring out how to stretch what they had. It put a lot of weight on me. I wanted to help in any way I could.

Every day after school my siblings and I had to wait in my mom's classroom for her to finish her lesson plans for the next day. While we waited we did our homework, so once we got home we could change into our play clothes and go outside. We played two-hand touch, hopscotch, and jump rope. Some days we sat on the steps of the building or on the playground and talked about things going on in school or the neighborhood.

Gangs and homicide were the top news stories just about every night. I can still recall my first encounter with them on the streets of Brooklyn. It was Friday, March 19th, we went on a school field trip to the Brooklyn Zoo. I'd never been there, and I loved it. Too bad my mom missed it she was really sick that day.

Which meant that once we got back to school there was no one to walk me, my brothers, my sister and friends home. Grams was at church, dad was at work, and Ms. Gloria didn't have a phone. We had no choice but to walk without adult supervision. The school wasn't far from our home, but it was the longest walk ever. We ran frantically, through the dark spots where the street lights had been knocked out. Once we got close enough to our house we thought we were safe. In our own neighborhood so we relaxed.

My brothers and our friends Shaun, Eric, and Jay went into the corner store a block from our house to get candy. I waited with Phalana and friends Teza, Randy, and Shay outside, against the wall. The boys came back with fruity Tootsie Rolls and quarter waters for everyone.

Unaware a lighter-skinned black man followed behind us as if he were in a rush. When he got closer we saw it was Mickey, a friend of our neighbor, Fred. We said hi to him, but he passed us as if we weren't there. We thought nothing of it and we continued playing around.

When Mickey was down the block a little, he attempted to cross the street until a brown Cadillac DeVille pulled up. Five guys got out. They had guns and were all dressed in black and face masks. None of them said a word to each other. They formed a circle around Mickey and fired round after round at him. Once they were done they kicked him to see if he was dead.

The other kids and I stood as still as streetlights, hoping not to be noticed. We'd witnessed a murder on our own block. I'd only ever seen anything like it on TV.

Once the guys in black were done they piled back into the car except for one. He walked toward us, looking around.

"Give me all your money!" he said as his friends yelled for him to leave us alone and get back in the car. My siblings and friends gave him everything they had, but I had to speak up. I made it clear I was not going to give him anything. I was afraid, but I knew how hard my parents worked to be able to give me a little extra change.

He was upset as he came closer to me, put the gun to my head, and said, "Do you want me to blow your brains out right here too."

I wasn't scared of him, but I didn't want to die. So I gave him what money I had. He walked away with the gun still pointed at us as if he were going to shoot anyway. He got in the car and it drove off. We just stood there, too scared to make any sudden moves.

Eventually we gathered ourselves and ran for our lives. My friend Shaun, who had really bad asthma, ran faster than I did. Ohaji grabbed my hand pulling me along, I was so afraid I couldn't nearly run fast enough. We all ran straight for our buildings, hoping the murderers hadn't noticed where we lived.

In the apartment my mother sat in the kitchen at the table, looking a mess. I could tell she wasn't feeling better, and she could tell something was up with us.

"Is everything okay?" she asked, trying to stand up.

"Yes, ma'am," Phalana said, her voice trembling. "Everything is fine. We were just seeing who could run the fastest."

My mom smiled. "I heard some gunshots. I didn't know if they were nearby."

We all shook our heads in response and quickly denied the rest of her questions. Ohaji again grabbed my wrist and we went to our room. We talked about what happened and pinky swore we wouldn't tell anyone. Once that was established my siblings yelled at me for getting smart with the man with the gun. I listened, and I agreed with everything they said but I really agreed just to be done with it. Honestly I knew that would be the last time my pride took a backseat for anyone.

As the next few days passed, we all went on with life. I had a few nightmares here and there.

It took two weeks before the local news station even acknowledged that there had been a murder in Brooklyn that night. Mickey's family wanted answers as to why he'd been murdered and why it hadn't been on the news. While eavesdropping on Mom and Ms. Gloria, I heard that the family had called on city officials to take more action in the search.

Our neighbor Fred, who had been Mickey's best friend, invited us to the funeral. Shaun, Phalana, Eric, and I went; no one else wanted anything to do with it. They didn't want to relive the whole thing or let Fred know we hadn't seen anything. Mom and Dad said it was okay for us to go. They trusted Fred he was our babysitter in the summertime when our parents both worked or wanted to be alone.

Fred suggested that we ride the train because the funeral was in the city. We were all silent the whole way. Fred's face was expressionless. He was unhappy, so none of us wanted to say much. Eric and Phalana sat there looking out the window and observing all the other passengers. Shaun and I played tic-tac-toe.

At least 200 people came out to pay their respects to Mickey. As we walked into the service, a girl in all black sang "I Told the Storm." Her voice was so good, it could have cleared away a hurricane. As her solo came to a close, four men in black approached the casket and fired rounds into it. Everyone fell to the floor in panic. I couldn't believe my eyes.

Before anyone in the service got the courage to do anything, the gunmen ran for the church's back door, and everyone else ran like crazy out the front. Fred yelled for us to grab hands and not let go. My mind replayed the night Mickey was murdered and I started crying uncontrollably. I wished I hadn't come. People were in complete shock. Mickey's family was at his casket, pleading on bended knee. We were trampling over one another to get to the subway.

I couldn't believe the gunmen got away again. That was enough to make me completely nervous, especially since I was still a little frightened of the gunman who had robbed us.

 I wanted to ask Fred so many questions that came to mind but I knew at the moment he wouldn't be able to find the words to answer. He looked down at the floor in shame the whole way home. My sister nudged my side as I began to ask a question. I sat back quietly for the rest of the trip.

Once we arrived home the funeral was all over the news. Fred apologized to our parents even though what happened wasn't his fault. Daddy made it clear we were not to attend anymore funerals in the city, especially not without him or Mom. Honestly I was okay with that.

Chapter 3

School slowly came to an end for the year. It was summer vacation and I was excited! Every summer each project building in Brooklyn had a barbeque. That meant free food. My siblings and I went to everyone's, Tupperware in hand. We'd have leftover food for weeks.

This summer would be memorable because it's the summer before my first year in high school and my best friend Shaun and I secretly started dating. Truth be told I wasn't allowed to date; according to my dad, my sister and I couldn't have boyfriends until after he died.

However my dad was really close to Shaun, so he didn't mind us dating once he found out.

Shaun was nice, smart and funny. Tall, athletic build and skin the color of caramel. He wasn't the most attractive as many girls would always say but he laughed at my corny jokes and I enjoyed his company. We were always close and we understood each other when no one else did. He always went out of his way to do nice things for me; he carried my books, he kept an extra jacket in his locker just in case I got cold or if I had forgotten mine, and he helped me with my homework. He was the perfect match for both my sarcasm and humor. I was a good match for his bluntness and arrogance.

Actually I had liked Shaun as more than my friend for a while. However my dad always said a woman should let the man make the first move. He said that when you make yourself to available to a man, regardless of whether or not he likes you, he'll take advantage of the opportunity. Dad also said allowing a man to make the first move makes him responsible for his future actions. I never understood my dad's thought. I just figured that maybe one day I would.

That summer marked another turning point in my life. I was tired of my family struggling to pay bills and supply the basics. Sharing clothes, barely having food, too ashamed and proud to ask others for help... I wanted new stuff and I wanted my parents not have to worry. So I got a part-time job as a bagger and cashier at the local grocery store. My parents were against my working and going to school, fearing my grades would drop. But after I kept begging them, they eventually said it was okay.

I was the youngest child in the family and the only one working. My brothers didn't have time to work due to their practice and game schedules. Phalana was too busy going to every dance audition in the state of New York and running the streets with her friends. Working was the last thing on her mind. Clearly I had no life.

I started at the grocery store in the middle of summer. I only got the job because I lied about my age and they really needed help. As the months went on I enjoyed the paydays. But I always somehow had to work when I could be having a good time with my friends. What made me hate it even more was the day I caught a lady and her kids stealing meat out of the freezer. I was walking down the aisle about to go to the back of the store, when I saw a lady slip a couple of sirloin steaks into her purse. I walked over to the lady and politely told her that I saw her stealing the steaks; of course she called me a liar. I ran to the store intercom and called for the store manager. She and her child took off running and I ran behind them, like a fool into the parking lot. I ran up to the car door to notice her reaching for something. It was a gun. My manager quickly backed down and ran inside to call the police. By the time the police showed up, she was gone. A by standing customer gave them her car tag number. I never saw that lady ever again and I am glad.

I wasn't pulling in enough money at the grocery store so I begged one of the local drug dealers to let me help him out. I began selling weed and running errands. As time went on I brought in a good amount of money. I knew it was wrong, but my family needed stuff, and I just kept telling myself it was temporary. I didn't know all that came with it because I was so young, and I didn't really care at the time.

I didn't sell in my neighborhood because I didn't want my parents to find out what I was doing. I came up with an idea to sell only to people who were functional addicts, so that I wouldn't feel as bad about it. Most of my clients were white, corporate people; nurses, lawyers, doctors, and people of higher status. They were also safer to deal with because they had so much to lose.

At first no one knew about my side hustle but my boyfriend Shaun. I tried to hide it, but soon my siblings found out and so did my parents. They almost killed me; especially my dad. I assured him it was only temporary. He was upset but he turned a blind eye only because I was helping out with the bills.

When anyone would ask where and how I got so much money, I would say I was just saving all I made at the grocery store. It became my cover up. My parents were hurt by my decision to sell drugs, but at the same time it helped make things a little easier for them. I didn't miss a day of class, or a Sunday at church. We had a little more money coming into the household for food and bills that we could actually pay tithes and eat out here and there.

I worked at the grocery store all through high school, remaining an honor roll student. I made sure I did everything as my parents wanted.

When I finished high school, I planned on going to college. There was no other option. Ohaji and Christian were already at the University of Southern California. My parents felt some sense of relief because they didn't have to worry about much; both had full scholarships and received monthly stipends. My brothers were not only athletes with scouts to back them up but straight A students as well. Ohaji played football and Christian played baseball, and both dreamed of playing professionally.

Ohaji, Christian, and Eric were the only guys in our group of friends to graduate from high school. All the other guys dropped out. Shaun began selling drugs for some quick cash in hopes to become a rapper. I thought it was stupid for him to drop out of school, but I supported his decision because I believed in his talent. Though I knew nothing about music, I would hang out with he and his friends would sometimes in the studio. I loved their drive so I would contribute money to help him make CDs to sell out of the back of his car.

Shaun went above and beyond on his music because he knew without a high school diploma it was going to be hard to make something of himself. I respected his ambition and dedication. But he needed to make something happen. He always stayed on me about going to college, his dreams for us and of me being his wife in the future.

High school graduation rolled around and I was the valedictorian of my class. My graduation day was also the same day Shaun got a call to sign with an established record label. Our families all went to dinner together to celebrate both of our accomplishments. Afterwards we went to a friend's graduation party. We stayed for about an hour, leaving early to go to my grandma's house; who wasn't at home. She was staying with my aunt for the weekend and I had a key.

Once we got there we talked for a while and eventually began kissing. That led to feeling and touching, and from there we had protected sex. I was a virgin up until that point and it was very painful. Blood was in the bed, so I had to wash the sheets so no one would know. That's all I want to share about that!

***

I decided to attend St. John's University to stay a little closer to home. My parents weren't happy at all; they wanted me to go to New York University.

We also decided to move in together. My parents weren't happy about it either nearly having a heart attack when I said I'd be living with Shaun. They only calmed down once we promised them we would get married eventually.

Shaun got a nice amount of advance money to work on his album and I still sold drugs and worked at the grocery store, so we were able to get a brownstone in a nicer area of Brooklyn. Shaun didn't want me to work at all, but I had other plans. I wanted to have My own business someday.

Chapter 4

When the holiday season came around Shaun and I were settled comfortably into our new place. I had also started undergrad classes at St. John's University. I worked at the grocery store on weekends and did work study through the school's library a couple days a week. On top of all that I still sold drugs. It sounds like a lot, but I had plenty of time for it all.

The drug business was good. I had a couple of people working under me and I traveled to different states to make sales. It seemed as my client base grew, I grew more addicted to the lifestyle it allowed me to have. There were many times I felt bad about what I was doing. I usually ignored those feelings because at the end of the day I felt like I needed the money, and I had to do what I had to do.

Around this time Shaun released his first album, surprisingly it went gold. I didn't really know what that meant, but when I found out I was excited because he was excited

"Congrats, baby," I said as he walked into the house from the studio.

"Thanks!"

He hadn't become an overnight household name, but he was on his way.

"How does it feel?" I asked, pouring us some wine to celebrate.

"It feels good, I guess. It really hasn't hit me yet." He put his feet up on the coffee table.

"I'm happy for you," I said as I sat on his lap.

"Thanks, Momma. That's why I love you." He leaned in to kiss me softly on my lips.

"Hmm, you're going to take over the world little by little." I was proud of him. He had done what he'd set out to do. He deserved it all.

"We're going to take over the world together. There's no me without you." He wrapped his arms around me and hugged me tight.

"I love you."

"I love you more."

***

Our excitement went on for months. However at some point things between us got a little strange. The more people acknowledged his accomplishments, the more we changed. Regular things like grocery shopping became to much. People stared at us and interrupted our dinner dates for autographs. I didn't see him as much as I used to because he was so busy. When I got a moment to spend with him, I wanted him all to myself. Apparently that was too much to ask.

I knew sooner or later I would have to realize that Shaun's success was going to be too much for us both. One night while attempting to get gas, two women approached him as I sat in the passenger's seat of the car.

"Hi, Shaun, how are you?" one of the young ladies said as she rubbed her hand across his back.

"Hi," he replied, glancing at me.

"You look even better in person," the other woman said leaning her flat butt and wide hips on my car.

"I'm good, ladies, pumping gas so my lady and I can catch a movie."

"Well, if you ever have time, I'd like to be in your movie."

I looked and listened as if I had no worries as Shaun replied to her, "I'm not talking about making a movie. I'm going to *see* one. Come on now my lady is in the car. You ladies have a good day."

Shaun put the gas pump back and opened the driver's side door. Before he could start the car up or I could say anything, the two ladies knocked on his window.

"Here's my number," the smaller one said, handing him a slip of paper. "You can reach either of us there at any time."

Really, I thought to myself.

"He won't need that," I said. "But thanks." I reached over Shaun, grabbed the paper out of the young woman's hand, and threw it out the passenger side window.

We never discussed this episode because I didn't see where he never made an attempt to make it clear he was taken. Yet after a while women like those two became an everyday battle. At times it was a little too much for me, that I found myself constantly questioning myself and our relationship. Not that I was insecure I just didn't know how to place my emotions. Though Shaun made every attempt to make it clear that regardless of how things changed, he wanted me by his side but his actions proved otherwise. The women got worse and the dynamic of our relationship changed. Before he would make sure he checked anyone who disrespected me. After awhile I had to fight him constantly to get him to even acknowledge that anything was wrong. The attention he was getting changed things, especially at the expense of my feelings.

Slowly he became less attentive. Then whenever we finally got a chance to be alone, his friends would show up and he'd completely ignore me. He would come home late at night or sometimes not at all. He'd lie, saying he'd been working in the studio later than expected; bringing gifts to make up for his mistakes. I turned a blind eye.

I wanted my old boyfriend back. I cried to my sister Phalana about it many nights. She always said he would come to his senses, that he was just being a man and that some day he would change. I just had to be patient. Basically telling me to settle for whatever I could get right now. The fame and the special treatment were a gift and a curse. As he became invincible, I became invisible. He changed, so I changed too. Though there were times I hated looking at myself in the mirror because I could see the change. I continued to hold on to something that made us both comfortable.

Waiting for things to go back to how they used to be, when I knew that would never happen. Things would get worse before they got better.

Chapter 5

"Shaun, this is Dila. Where are you and why aren't you returning my calls? It's our anniversary and I had plans for us. Call me. Tell me something."

I left a teary message on his cell phone. It was our ninth year anniversary and he was nowhere to be found. I'd made dinner, bought him a new watch, and dressed really sexy.

All for him to call me back three hours later, when dinner was cold and I'd finished the whole bottle of wine by myself. "Hey, Momma. Sorry I missed your call. I had a show in Philly. I know it's our anniversary and I hate that I can't spend it with you."

"I understand." That was a lie. I was hurt, but I didn't want to admit. I didn't want him to feel like I disapproved of his career. But it gets in the way of everything.

"I'll make it up to you when I get back. I promise."

"Don't worry about it. There's always next year," I said, trying to convince myself that things would be different. At that point I should've known better. We hung up the phone and I spent the entire night crying.

The next day I was in the library, working on a term paper, when I overheard two women on the other side of a shelf talking about their night.

"Girl, last night was so much fun. Shaun came through and he hung out with us. He spent the night and made me breakfast this morning."

She paused as all the other ladies ooh'd and aah'd. I listened closely, wondering if she was referring to my Shaun.

"Did you sleep with him? How was it?" another girl asked.

"Girl, it was so good. But I'm not telling you details." The girl said excited to share with her friend. "He took me out to dinner at Baisen, this nice five star Cajun restaurant. We had several glasses of wine, talked about our dreams and things we'd love to do. Then we left and went back to my place. He wasn't going to come at first; something about he needed to get home to a girlfriend. But I told him that I'd promise to make it worth his while if he stayed." The friend then interrupted, "Go on." She continues, "He sat down on the couch as I freshened up and slipped into this to cute lingerie set I had bought but never wore. Girl, he didn't know what to do with himself as I began to kiss him and take off his clothes at the same time! We had sex on my living room floor. It was good." Both girls giggled as if they knew I was his girlfriend and that I was listening. "Wow, at least someone had a good night. I was laid out in my bed waiting for my new friend to come and he never showed up. Men are such a waste sometimes." The taller friend said as she stood to her feet. "Girl yes they are but last night was so not a wasted one." They both walked off and I quickly gathered my things to leave the library.

When I got home Shaun was sitting on the sofa, eating Chinese takeout from a box. I stood over him upset.

"What's up?" he said after hearing me walk in the front door.

"How was your show last night?" I asked, trying to put the pieces of the library story together.

"It was good. I killed it," he replied, not once acknowledging my obvious irritation.

"I bet you did! What did you do after?" I continued the conversation. "Nothing me and the guys went to get some late night food and chilled at the studio all night talking and hanging out. Why?" he asked. "I just asked, because it was our anniversary and I guess I assumed that it would be more important than anything else either of us had going on." I replied taking off my shoes. "I wasn't with another woman Phadila. If that is what you are implying." He replied annoyed. "I didn't say it. You did, so it must've been true. You went to Baisen and to some chicks house?" I replied pissed. "No I didn't. I was where I told you. You can call the guys to ask if you want." He handed me the phone. "No need, all they'll do is lie for you." I stormed out of the living room into the bedroom as he replied, "This shit getting old Phadila. You accusing me of things I have not done". I slammed the bedroom door.

I left it alone. I knew he would lie and I knew as always it would all come out eventually.

And it did, months later. I found out that he was indeed laid up with some girl across town on our anniversary. He left his phone on the night stand one night and I decided to look through his old messages and emails. Whether or not she was the girl from the library I didn't know. But what I do know is he was not being honest to me or faithful and the words "I love you" were just that; words. After crying myself to sleep that night I could feel that I was slowly growing emotionally distant. I could no longer turn the other cheek and act like I didn't deserve better.

I shouldn't be with someone and feel jealous of his hoes. His hoes should be jealous of me. Before the fame chicks weren't checking for him. I didn't understand and the more we would argue the more I'd vent to family and friends. They always told me to stay with him and that it was just a phase. Everyone except my Grams—she encouraged me to take a break while Shaun figured out what he wanted.

"Everybody has a limit," she always said. I guess I hadn't reached mine yet and even though I'm feeling the way I am. I still didn't want to break up.

Nights confused, angry, and alone had become my new lifestyle. I stopped going to Shaun's shows and caring what was going on with him just so I wouldn't get hurt anymore. One of his biggest shows to date was on a Wednesday night and I had an early class the next morning. At first I wasn't going to go, but my sister talked me into it. When I arrived there were people everywhere and half-naked women at easy disposal. I went into Shaun's dressing room and there he was, getting oral pleasure from some random chick. I guess *private* was the perfect word for his room. I felt like someone had stabbed me in the heart. I flipped out, grabbed the girl by her hair, and pulled her to her feet.

"What the hell is going on?" She shouted.

"Get out!" I shouted, and then I turned to Shaun. "So this is what you do? Did it cross your mind that I may show up?"

He quickly pulled up his pants and fixed his clothes.

"Do you hear me?" I pushed him twice. I got no response, so I pushed him again.

He jumped up and grabbed me by my neck. "Have you lost your mind?" He squeezed my neck so tightly I was nearly blue in the face. I struggled to get loose.

"Shaun, ten minutes 'til you're expected onstage," a female voice said through the door as he continued to hold my neck tight. As the voice trailed off in the distance, he released me, fixed his clothes, took a sip of his drink, and walked out as if nothing had happened. I sat on his dressing room floor for a few minutes to pull myself together.

I left driving straight to my Gram's house for comfort.

"Grams, I went to the show and he and some girl were in his dressing room together." I told her the story in tears. She sat on the sofa and listened to every word. "Then he grabbed me by my neck. I couldn't breathe."

"Phadila, calm down. We can talk about it in the morning when your mind is clear." Grams hugged me tightly, leading me upstairs. "Go to sleep. We'll talk over breakfast."

I lay in bed crying for hours. Just as my eyes began to close, Shaun called my cell phone.

"Phadila," he said, "please let me talk to you."

I didn't say a word.

"I'm so sorry," he continued. I hung up.

"Phadila, Shaun's outside," Grams said a short while later, knocking on the door. I dashed to the window to see him sitting outside in his car. After he called Grams's house phone two or three more times, I went down to hear what he had to say. My face was red as blush and puffy from crying. He got out opening the passenger's door for me, and I got in. The apologies started before he was even back in the car.

"Phadila, I was wrong. I was so out of it. I was just so shocked when I actually saw you that I didn't know how to react. I promise it won't ever happen again. I was drinking and smoking. I wasn't in my right mind."

I couldn't even look at him. "How could you do that to me? First you missed our anniversary and lied about having a show, now this? We've been together too long for this crap, Shaun. What are you thinking? Better yet, *are* you thinking?"

"Dila, I'm sorry. I just…"

"You are very sorry and weak."

"Look, I love you. I would never leave you. We've built too much together for that even to be a thought. Things happen, and I promise I will do better. I promise."

He grabbed my chin to kiss me. I turned my head, allowing him to kiss my cheek.

I folded my arms uninterested. "So I'm supposed to sit around and be treated like crap while you do whatever?"

"I promise, Dila. No more messing around. I promise I'll do better."

I looked up and made eye contact with him and at that moment I couldn't think of anything better than being with him . Maybe I was dumb but I quickly forgave him and we left Gram's to head home.

Chapter 6

Over the next few days Shaun was back to his old self and I was back to being head over heels in love. He did the things he used to do like buying me flowers for no reason, spending time with me, and listening to me talk about whatever was on my mind. He listened to my thoughts even when I made no sense. I had my man's back and I was happy.

Of course it didn't take long for rumors of him messing with other women to resurface, but I ignored them because he showed no signs of stepping out. He treated me like I was the only woman for him therefore; I went on with my everyday life.

My senior year in college finally came around just as Shaun was preparing to release his second album. To celebrate my graduation, Phalana and my best friend Randy treated me to a mani and pedi.

"Thanks for this, guys," I said, watching my feet soak. "I really appreciate it. It feels so good to be pampered."

"Girl, anytime. You deserve it," Randy replied. "We're all college graduates now. So what are we going to do?"

"That's a good question. I have no idea," said my sister.

"I think I want to go to law school and become a lawyer." I blew the nail polish on my hands.

"That sounds like a lot of extra work. I'll pass.," said Phalana.

"Well yeah," Randy added. "We'll leave all that to you." We all giggled.

"I want to do business law. That would be really cool." I continued.

"Hm," said Phalana. "Yea that would be best for you. Lord knows you need not to be an entertainment lawyer. I'm sure Shaun wouldn't like you cock blocking his game."

"Ooh," Randy said with a smirk. "Phadila, you're a good woman. I personally couldn't handle it if my man had a weakness for other women like that." I drew a blank as my mood began to shift a bit. I wasn't sure where this conversation was about to go.

"Well, at least you don't have to worry about him leaving," Phalana went on. "Regardless of how many women he messes with, he's in love with you and that's all that matters."

I knew she was trying to make my situation sound better, but it just sounded disgusting. I couldn't say a word. My relationship with Shaun had not been okay, but it was mine! We were doing better and I didn't really want to joke about this right now. I wanted to enjoy being pampered.

Two hours later we gathered our things to leave. On my way out the door I bumped into another lady accidentally who was coming through the door.

"Excuse me," I said.

"You're excused," she replied with an unnecessary attitude.

I was not amused. "On second thought, I take that back." Randy, Phalana, and I continued out.

"Phadila you should've went upside her head. Old dumb ho," Randy joked.

"Phadila?" The woman laughed, "Shaun's girlfriend Phadila? You can't be serious. *I'm* not the dumb one." She stepped outside of the door to respond.

"What business is it of yours?" I turned to ask.

"It's not, but your man is my business every now and then."

"Oh, really. Well I'm sure he can't be too fulfilled by you. You don't even fill out your jeans."

The woman walked away. "Tell him thanks," she said over her shoulder. "I needed this pedicure."

I didn't know how to react but Phalana did. She threw a glass bowl and hit the lady dead in her face.

"Don't you ever in your life talk to my sister that way! He may fuck you or give you twenty dollars to get your feet done, but you won't ever be wifey you ole dusty, two-cent ho!" She pulled out her wallet. "And here's twenty more dollars. Maybe you'll get that knot on your head taken care of." Randy cracked up laughing as I stood there a little hurt.

We then got into my car, and drove off.

"Phalana, you are officially crazy," Randy said from the backseat. "I mean, I already figured you were, but that right there just made it all clear. You're crazy!"

Neither Phalana nor I responded. I was upset, and my sister could read it all over my face. She reached over to hold my hand as I drove.

By the time we reached my house, I had cooled off a little. Then, just as I pulled in the driveway, I got a call.

"Hi, Dila." It was Chuck, one of my runners. "I was wondering if we could meet up and talk. There was an incident with a client yesterday and I just want to discuss it with you."

"Can we talk about it right now over the phone?" I asked. "I'm really tired." I felt funny about meeting him because my instinct was telling me something was up. But I decided to meet anyway.

"My minutes on my phone don't start until after nine. I'd rather just talk about it now and get it over with. It won't take long," he pressed. "Can we meet at Junior's in downtown Brooklyn?"

"Okay. But I can't stay long."

I let my sister and Randy out to get into their own cars as I pulled out of the driveway to head to Junior's. It was getting gloomy and cold out, which made me regret my decision to meet up with Chuck even more. I wanted to be home so I could deal with the issue of this girl and her pedicure.

When I got to Junior's I drove around the block to scope out the scene. Something told me this meeting wasn't right, and I wanted to make sure I came out alive. I parked the car two blocks over just so Chuck wouldn't notice me coming if he indeed had something planned. I only trusted him as far as I could throw him.

I reached in my glove compartment and got my pistol. I put it in my waistband. I'm not a huge fan of guns, but until it was time to leave this lifestyle alone, I kept it. I actually had never used it.

Chuck was waiting outside the restaurant with two guys. As I peeked around the corner at them, I got this funny feeling. I called his phone.

"You know what?" I told him. "Maybe tomorrow, I'm just not up for it today." I had a hunch this was a setup, and my instinct never failed me.

"What?" he replied. "Come on, today or never."

Just as I backed away to walk back to my car, one of the guys with Chuck pointed to me. I ran as fast as I could as the three of them were right on my heels.

"Freeze or I'll shoot!" a voice said. At that moment I knew my instinct was right.

A tall, slim, white police officer searched my body. "Phadila Lombardijones," he said as he patted me down. "We've been watching you for almost a year. It's nice to finally catch up with you and take you down. Prison and disobeying the law seems to run in your family."

He found my pistol the only bit of evidence at the moment, but he made it clear he had enough to send me away for a long time. He forced me into the backseat of a cruiser and drove me downtown, where I was booked on charges; Possession, trafficking, attempt to sale and delivery. There was nothing I could do, even though I had nothing on me that very day. They had been keeping a watchful eye on me and all I could do was request my one phone call.

"Hi Daddy," I paused. I was afraid to tell him.

"Hi, love. What's going on?"

"Dad, I'm in jail."

Silence filled the empty space in the phone. I could feel his anger and disappointment.

"What do you mean you're in jail?" he finally asked. "What happened? I thought you said you stopped." He rattled off questions. I could hear my mom stressing in the background.

"I know. I lied. One of my runners set me up. I'm sorry, Dad. I really am."

"Phadila, why?" My mom had taken the phone from Dad.

"Mom, I'm sorry. I'm going to need you guys to bail me out. I know I'm more than likely going to have a trial because they have been watching me. So I want to talk to the whole family before anything happens."

"You be careful in there until we do."

I smiled. My mom's response relaxed me just a bit. "I will," I replied, hanging up the phone.

Another officer put me in a holding cell, and I stayed there for twenty-four hours until my family paid my half a million dollar bail. Weeks later my trial date was set.

I felt that I owed my family and friends an apology and an explanation. Most of my family knew I had been arrested and many of them weren't surprised. My parents had already set up a meeting at my grandma's house so I could talk to everyone all at once. The car ride to Grams's however was silent. I didn't know what to say to my parents and they didn't know what to say to me.

Once everyone arrived at Grams's, the questions started before I could even find a seat.

"What's going on? And where did you get all that money you had in the safe?" My aunt Linda asked.

"I made it and I've been saving it over time," I replied looking at my parents who had used that money to bail me out.

"How could you do this to our family?" Aunt Freda asked. "We've worked so hard for all of you kids to have a good life. You just graduated from college. You were talking about law school. What are you doing?"

"This isn't about the family," I told her. "This is about me and my choice to continue doing something I knew could land me in this situation. I just wanted to make sure my family never wanted for anything. I was tired of struggling, and apparently some of you were too you always came straight to me for money. I didn't spend it alone. No one ever asked then where I got it from when they needed to borrow some."

I continued to answer their questions, but I was annoyed. "My choice was dumb," I finally said, "but I don't regret it."

I tried not to catch my dad's eye. I knew what he'd gone through growing up, and he'd never wanted his kids to be associated with the streets. He was more upset than anyone in the room. "You lied to me, Phadila," he said, his voice low. "You said you were done. I just don't understand. I told you guys about all the things I saw in my family. I tried to keep you out of the fire, and you still got mixed up in it."

My brother Christian stepped in. "Hold on everyone. She was trying to do what she could to help out our family. I'm not mad at all. I just wish maybe you had put your energy into something else to make money. But I can't be mad because she helped Mom and Dad put food in our mouths. She paid bills and made sure we had things we needed and wanted. What can any of us really say because she's helped many of us in some kind of way?"

"I guess Christian is right," Dad said. "I just wish you'd discussed it with your mother and me.

The room was silent far beyond just a moment. Most of my family didn't want to say much because I had helped them out financially on several occasions. My grandma, though, did not hold her tongue.

"I'm not upset with you or disappointed one bit," she said, stepping from behind the kitchen counter. Everyone in the room sat up a little straighter. "You used what you knew to help those around you. You are a very intelligent human being. There is nothing selfish about what you've done for this family. In my eyes your actions speak volumes. I admire you for your heart. But you will have to do the time for what you've done. At the end of the day it was illegal. Just hold your head high and ask God for his grace and mercy."

Grams stood there looking at me as everyone gathered in a circle for prayer. For the rest of the night I sat in the corner, alone and in silence. I was upset with myself and embarrassed for my family. They didn't deserve to be put to shame.

"Phadila," Dad said, coming over to me. "I'm upset. But I'll make sure I do everything in my power to get you out of this."

"Thanks Dad," I said. "I love you and I'm sorry."

After that meeting the days rolled away. I spent a lot of time with my family though I knew it would make this experience harder to deal with.

Chapter 7

After the trial I was sentenced to thirty years in prison with the possibility of parole. I wasn't sure how I would survive in prison, but I knew I had better figure it out.

"New booty, ladies!" a woman shouted as I walked past her cell. Two guards escorted me down the hall to my new place of residence: cell block B. The very minute the bars closed behind me, I knew it was a losing game and there was no time for tears.

My first four months in I spent by myself. I always sat in the same spot in the courtyard, on the bench farthest from everyone else.

"What's up with you, pretty girl? Are you too good for the rest of us?" one of them asked. She was husky and mean.

"Nah, I ain't ever too good. I just prefer being alone, that's all." She made me a bit nervous.

"I understand that sometimes, but all the time? What's your name?"

I looked up at her. "Phadila."

She motioned for me to move over so she could take a seat.

"Phadila. That's cute. I'm Candace. Why are you in here, young blood?"

Though I really didn't feel like talking to Candace, I knew I was going to have to make a friend or two to keep my sanity.

"Trafficking, weapon charges, and other stuff that all means the same thing," I replied.

She giggled. "So true, They just find different ways of saying it to make us look even worse."

I shrugged my shoulders in response.

"How long did you get?"

"Thirty with the possibility of parole, You?"

She looked around as if it were a secret. "Man, I'll be in here for the rest of my life. I murdered my husband." She sounded kind of proud of her actions.

"Damn, what did he do?"

"He used to beat me all the time until I was black and blue in the face. I got fed up. He hit me one night and I stabbed him to death."

I felt bad for Candace. She probably felt safer in jail, with her husband dead, than she did with him.

After that day Candace and I became friends. She stood up for me when someone wanted to fight me, which I appreciated because I didn't want to fight anyone. I didn't want to mess up my behavior in any way because I wanted every chance I had to get out.

* * *

As the months went on, sleeping became harder and harder. Hearing people scraping their toothbrushes on the floors at night to make weapons and cellmates pleasuring each other for the sake of sanity kept me awake. Usually I didn't get to sleep until it was nearly time for breakfast.

"Get up! Breakfast!" The guard would yell every morning. I would drag myself out of bed and wait for my cell door to open.

"How are you today?" Candace approached me as I went through the food line.

"I'm good." I wasn't in the mood to talk.

"This is Tina." She pointed to the woman behind her in line. "She was brought in last night. She's my cellmate."

"Nice to meet you, Tina," I said.

"Likewise," Tina replied.

We all proceeded to sit at our usual table.

"Did you read that book I gave you a couple days ago?" Candace asked.

"Yeah, I did. Thanks. It was really good." I replied.

"It's one of my favorite books ever." Candace continued. "Reading keeps me sane in this place."

We made small talk through breakfast and then in the courtyard afterward. Tina said she was in for killing her pimp. I didn't ask for any further details. She killed someone; I figured that was all I needed to know.

Time seemed to fly by but I wasn't happy until I started getting my visitation rights. I also loved attending the church service on Sundays. Usually after service I would talk to the pastor to make sense of his sermons. This particular day he was speaking about how God loves everyone in spite of the things they do. It made me realize though I sold drugs and I feel like I should've stopped when I had the chance to. I couldn't be forgiven for what I had done.

"Pastor Johnson, do you know how it's possible for one man to love everyone so much and still not judge them by their actions?" I asked the prison Pastor one Sunday after service.

"Well, God is love, and he loves unconditionally. What you do, what you say, and your attempts to prove who you are to people are all loveable functions. Nothing is unlovable in God's eyes."

Even though I was locked in a cage and treated like I was an animal with no freedom. God still found a reason to love me. It wasn't unbelievable I had been to church many times in my life and I believed in God to some extent. I was just at a point where I wanted to make better sense of who God was.

To keep my mind busy I read books and I wrote letters every week to family and friends. I wrote to Shaun, but he never wrote back, and I never asked why as long as he showed up every other Saturday to visit. Seeing him meant more to me than getting letters from him.

That morning I got as cute as I could in my orange jumper and rushed out the double doors to see his face.

"Phadila!" he said.

"Shaun, hi!" I ran into his arms and kissed him. "I missed you."

"I missed you too."

"You smell so good." I sniffed and sniffed as we walked hand in hand to the nearest table.

We sat down across from each other. "I'm glad you came today. I really need to talk to you about some stuff."

"You do?"

"Yeah. I've been here for a short time and I feel like I have been selfish and I think we should just be friends so you can live your life without worrying about me."

"Are you sure about that?"

I bowed my head. "I'm not, but it's the best thing."

He grabbed hold of my chin and kissed my lips softly. It sent a chill down my spine. I hadn't realized how much I missed his touch.

"If that's what you feel we need, then that's what it is. I'm not going to fight with you." He replied but something inside of me told me that he had already moved on. "So how is everything? Anything new?" I asked.

"Everything is good. I'm on tour now and we've been to a lot of places." He took an envelope from his pocket and showed me photos of his trips.

"Oh my goodness, You met LL Cool J?" LL had been my first crush.

"Yea, I did. He's really cool. I told him how much you were in love with him, posters all over the wall and all."

We both laughed at the memory. Back then our lives were a little less complicated.

"Shaun, I'm so proud of you. You're living your dream."

"Thanks, Dila. I wish I could experience it all with you."

We made eye contact just before an awkward silence.

"Well, sometimes God's plans are a little different than what we've planned," I said, wishing I could be out there with him.

"Visitation is over," yelled a guard in the corner of the room. "Everyone please line up."

Shaun and I squeezed in a last hug "bye," I said watching him walk out. The guard brought us back to our cells for the evening.

"Psst. Lombardi," Candace called from her cell once we were locked back in.

"Yeah." I rested my forehead on the bars.

"Your boyfriend is cute. How long have you guys been together?"

"Since we were thirteen I think I stuck my foot in my mouth because I told him today I don't want him to wait on me. I want him to move on with his life." My heart jumped into my throat as I repeated the conversation in my head.

"Why would you do that? You're going to get out of here sooner than the rest of us. File an appeal and make it happen. Get back to your man and your life."

I smiled. Why didn't Candace ever take her own advice? "How do I file an appeal?"

"Talk to your lawyer. He'll make it all happen for you."

Candace was right. Which is why when I met with my lawyer the following week, I requested him to appeal my case. By the time Saturday morning came around I was excited as I walked into in the visiting room, where my parents waited with my attorney Mr. Issac.

"Phadila," he said, shaking my hand.

"Mr. Isaac, thank you for coming." I replied, "Mom, Dad." I felt myself turning into that four-year-old girl who used to cry when her parents left for work. They embraced me in a hug and I melted right into their arms.

"How are you holding up" my mom asked. "I'm good." I replied. "It's cool." I replied. "Mr. Isaac, I want to do an appeal on my case. Is that possible?" I stated very quickly.

"That's definitely possible, Phadila. I'll talk to a few other people and we'll come together to make it happen."

That response was everything I needed to hear. He ran down the details and steps of the process as myself and parents took notes. After that we talked about things going on in jail, which was not much. It felt so good to see my parent's faces and hold them in my arms even if it wasn't for long.

As I went back to my cell, I was left with so many emotions I couldn't explain. I sat on my cot thinking about the appeal and all it entailed. It would be a process, but I was ready for it.

Chapter 8

The months rolled on, each day no different from the last. Every morning I was woken up by a guard but this morning was different.

I lay on my cot daydreaming as I was interrupted by the guard. "The warden wants to speak with you."

"For what?" I asked, but he never replied. He placed shackles on my arms and my ankles as if I were a dead man walking. He took me down the hall around the corner on the other side of the prison to a small room with a table and two chairs.

"Sit down." The guard turned to leave.

As I sat down, millions of thoughts ran through my head. Unsure of what was going on, I put my forehead on the table to ease my mind just a little. A short, chunky, white male entered with a folder in his hand. He got closer than I had realized it was Police Chief Toms.

"Phadila Lombardijones," he said, pulling out his chair.

"Ugh," I thought as I just ahead not saying a word. He was a known asshole.

"Do you know why you're in here?" he asked.

"Why?" I asked, hoping he would get to the point.

"You're in this room because I need your help." He put the folder on the table and opened it. I sat quietly, waiting. "You're here because a lot of your clients are very prominent people in the city of New York. We're trying to crack down on people because they are making people like me look bad."

"Trust me you need no help looking bad." I replied sarcastically. Chief smiled replying, "So what do you have to tell me Phadila?"

"Well, sir, what people do in their private lives isn't my business to tell."If he wanted to investigate someone himself that's fine with me but I wasn't going to tell him a thing and he knew that. I wasn't going to be involved in the loss of people's careers, families, or respect.

"This isn't the time to be a smartass."

I leaned on the table. "This also isn't the time to ask me any questions, about something I'm not going to answer."

"Listen here! I don't have time for your games. There are people who need to be exposed, and most of them were clients of yours. Now either you tell me or you will be punished."

He was upset and I really didn't care. "I understand you want to bring some people down so you can look like a savior. Well, sir, some of the people you're trying to expose are your very own friends, and friends of mine. Who, by the way, have told me some very disturbing things about you too. Things you may not want to be uncovered. Things dealing with under aged children. I mean if we're exposing I say let's expose."

He looked upset and ashamed. He apparently hadn't expected me to know about his infatuation with little boys. Oh, but I did, and if he thought for one minute exposing my clients wasn't going to get him exposed, he had another thing coming.

"Listen to me and listen well," he said, pointing a finger at me. "If you ever speak of those lies about me again I will have you killed."

"Mr. Toms, you listen to me and you listen to me well. If you ever threaten my life again, you won't have time to kill me because I'll kill you first. And if you ever attempt to question me on anything outside of how my day is going, I will show proof of what you're claiming is lies. Are we done?" I rose out of my seat. The guard came back in and took me to my cell. That was the last time Mr. Toms or anyone questioned me about my clients or anything else for that matter.

* * *

Before I realized it, I'd made it through the first year and a half of my prison term. Every day just rolled into the next. I was actually a bit excited because I had received my appeal letter from the state of New York and my request had finally been approved. The date had been set for next month and if God saw fit, I would have a second chance at freedom. The only catch was if I were released, I would be on parole for the next ten years and would have to report it to any job I applied to.

I was full of joy from the letter and also excited about seeing my sister's pregnant belly. I got dressed to go out and greet them, rushing through the double doors.

My mom and sister were all smiles. But the expression on Shaun's face was entirely different. Something was wrong. I hugged my mom and my sister while rubbing her belly.

"I'm going to be an auntie!" I said. "This is so exciting!"

As excited as I was, I couldn't take my eyes off of Shaun's expression. He hugged me different, it felt very empty but I tried to pay it no mind as we all sat at the table. The more I glanced at him the more he hung his head.

"Phadila, I miss you," Phalana said.

"I miss you guys too. But you will not believe the good news I have."

"She got her appeal!" my mom shouted.

"Dang, Mom, I wanted to tell them," I said.

"Well, baby, you were taking too long. I've been praying for this for a while now." I let my mom have her moment. I still couldn't get over Shaun's mood.

"What's up? What's wrong?" I asked him.

"I have to give you some news as well," he said. "Before anyone else tells you." He looked to catch my mom's and sister's expressions. I sat up straight in my seat nervous.

"I'll get right to it," he said. "So Phadila, I…I have a baby on the way."

The words sent my brain into complete overload. I couldn't believe what I was hearing. I stared off into space, trying to act as if I hadn't heard what had just happened. I didn't want to let them all see that my joy had been stolen. I gasped for air to say.

"Congrats," My voice shaking. "What are you having?"

"A boy, and we're planning on naming him Justin."

I went into yet another panic. That was the name we'd said we'd name our baby if we ever had one. My face was damn near in flames as I fought off the tears.

"That's a nice name," I said calmly. I sat in a brief silence as my mom, sister, and Shaun talked about everything that was going on in the outside world. I heard nothing. My mind weaved in and out of the conversation. But that moment felt like the longest moment of my life.

Just as the conversation turned back to me, the guard announced visitation was over for the day. We said our goodbyes and I went back to my cell. I sat on my cot replaying Shaun's announcement in my head. Growing angrier with myself for not reacting the way I really wanted to even though I really had no right because we were no longer a couple. I thought us separating while I was locked up would make sense but now that he's found someone else, I regret the decision. I cried myself to sleep that entire night and every time it crossed my mind thereafter.

* * *

On the day of my appeal I walked into the courtroom with chains on my wrists and ankles and guards at my sides. I was embarrassed. All my family and friends were there for support. At 10:00 on the dot in walked Judge Ferguson, who was also one of my previous clients. I wasn't sure of how this all would play out, but damn it, I hoped it would work in my favor.

As my lawyer presented my side of the case, I prayed to calm my spirits. The appeal went on for an hour. I paid attention to everything that was said, taking notes here and there.

"Ms. LombardiJones is a criminal by courtroom standards," Mr. Isaac the opposing lawyer said at one point. "She's no different from any other drug dealer, pimp, or hoodlum on the streets. Her clientele was upper class, but she still ran an illegal organization."

I got a little upset at their argument. He was making me out to be someone I wasn't and it really bothered me. I didn't kill anyone. I didn't do anything wrong besides sell drugs to functional people. I felt like interrupting his speech and giving him a piece of my mind. But I remained cool. I'm sure I'll have my chance to speak.

My lawyer stood to the floor and gave a few words as, Judge Ferguson leaned forward. "Ms. Lombardijones, is there anything you want to say in response?"

I looked at my parents for validation, holding my head high as I stood to speak.

"I would like to say thank you, Judge Ferguson, for this moment. I really appreciate it. What I do not appreciate is who I've been made out to be in this court. It's completely invalid. It's disheartening to see people rip me apart just to add another win to their resume. I am a person of empathy, courage, and strength, and I live in fear of no one but God. Nothing I did previously, as stated here in this courtroom, was with the intent to harm anyone. All I wanted was a better life for my family. My choices weren't the best, but just like these lawyers, I did what I felt I needed to for a win. I was doing what I could at my age to help make things easier for my parents, who didn't deserve struggling to feed their children. They're good people. I did things the best way I knew how, coming from my neighborhood. However, if given another chance, I can and will be a great citizen. I apologize. I meant no real harm."

As I sat down, I wasn't sure if what I'd said was good or bad. The courtroom remained quiet. But God was all over me I could feel his presence.

Judge Ferguson called for a recess to make his decision. I was allowed to mingle with my family and friends. We prayed and enjoyed each other's company. About thirty minutes later, the judge walked back into the courtroom. We all stood to our feet as he sat glancing at the faces around the room.

"I have made my decision." He said continuing, "We the court and the State of New York have decided to grant Ms. Phadila Lombardijones an overturn in her case."

My heart stopped. Had I heard him right? I thought. Cheers of joy erupted all around me.

"Silence in the court!" Judge Ferguson shouted.

Tears rolled down my cheeks as I looked up to God and mouthed, "Thank you."

"Furthermore, Ms. Lombardijones," the judge continued, "you will serve two years, most of which you have already served. You will have parole for the next five years, and since you enjoy helping others you will have two thousand hours of community service. I wish you luck, and I don't want to see your face in my courtroom ever again."

He picked up his paperwork and got up to leave.

I felt like a huge weight had been lifted off of my shoulders. I took several deep breaths and laid my forehead on the table in relief. A guard nudged me so that he could begin escorting me back to my cell. No one could tell me anything as I glided down the hall, full of joy. Yet again God had made the unthinkable possible.

When I reached my cell, I fell to my knees with tears in my eyes. "Lord, I come to you with honor and praise in my heart. You've made what seemed impossible possible. I have to say thank you! With this second chance I will make sure I walk on a straight and narrow path. I want to teach others not to make the same mistake and lead by example of the greatness you possess. I give you my life, my soul, my spirit, and my belief that you are God above all. Amen."

I sat for a few minutes and I cried as I thought of my life ahead of me. Once I pulled myself together, I reached for a shoe box under my cot and pulled out a black Sharpie. On the cell wall I wrote:

> (9) And he said unto me, my grace is sufficient for thee: for my strength is made perfect in weakness. Most gladly therefore will I rather glory in my infirmities, that the power of Christ may rest upon me.
>
> (10) Therefore I take pleasure in infirmities, in reproaches, in necessities, in persecutions, in distresses for Christ's sake: for when I am weak, then am I strong.

That night, for the first time in nearly two years, I slept well.

Chapter 9

"I told you," Candace said, hip bumping me in the lunchroom line the next afternoon.

"You did. Thanks. I couldn't have done it without your support."

"Girl, it wasn't me. It was God, and if I ever hear you giving me any kind of praise I'm going to smack your ass."

We both laughed. "Candace, I'm going to miss you. You've made my days here better. You're my only friend in the pen."

"Anytime. I like showing people the way because I never had anyone to show me anything. I'm happy for you. But promise me that when you walk out that door, you'll never look back. That means no letters or contacting any of us. The past will be the past. This moment is happening for a reason. Use it to move on."

I was confused. "So you won't want to be my friend when I'm a free woman?"

"Far from the truth but when you're living a life for something greater than yourself, you have to know when to let go of people and things that keep you from being what God intended. It's not by chance your life happened the way it did. There's a greater reason, and if any of us were in your life we'd hold you back. Our purpose was to show you what someone never showed us and let you go."

Though I didn't agree with forgetting her, Candace made sense. We sat there enjoying our lunch until it was time to go back to our cells. The days dwindled until I was down to my last two weeks. Saturday, July 29 would be my last day in prison. I was more a little more excited for my last visitation. My parents and Shaun were waiting when I walked out and my stomach turned when I saw his smiling face. I was excited to see him, but at the same time I was still upset.

Judging from the way Mom and Dad hugged me so tight, I figured they were as excited to see me. They wasted no time on spilling the beans on everyone's business. I guessed they wanted to lighten the shock I would feel when I was released. Shaun followed suit, telling me that his son had been born earlier that week. He even showed me pictures. My temper boiled. I quickly changed the subject.

"Two more weeks, I'm so excited!" I said. Shaun fell back. He had caught my intent.

"We're all excited," Mom said, smiling wide. "Dad's going to pick you up that morning."

"That's cool. The first things I need are chicken, cornbread, and wine. Not in that order." Thoughts of anything and everything possible crossed my mind.

We talked more about the world outside of my cage, and I got more and more excited about my release. The guard soon returned to escort me back to my cell, and we all said our farewells. I walked away unwillingly but knew we'd see each other again soon.

The last two weeks went by so quickly I couldn't keep up.

"Dila, you'll be out of here tomorrow. Lucky you!" Candace shouted through the bars of her cell.

"I know. I'm excited! I have so much to do and catch up on." I had the biggest smile on my face.

"Don't be like the rest of them and end up back in here. Make a difference," Said another inmate to my left.

"I will, I promise!" I couldn't believe I had spent the last two years of my life in prison. I stood there replaying how I'd gotten there, start to finish.

"Lights out," the guard yelled down the hall. I rose from the cold, concrete floor and sat on my cot. I was too excited to sleep.

A voice in another cell said, "You don't deserve to be here. You're not one of us."

"Thank you," I replied.

I laid on my cot for hours. When I finally began to doze off the guard was at my cell, waking me up for the signing out process. I missed breakfast and didn't even shower. I didn't really care too much since I was leaving.

I quickly gathered myself and didn't look back. There was so much paperwork; I couldn't remember signing that much when I first had been brought into prison. But I had no complaints I was leaving. When the door to the outside world opened, I swear the sun shined so bright it was a little too much to handle. But I was happy. I skipped out and over to my Dad, who waited with Ohaji and Christian. We all fell into the biggest and longest group hug ever.

"Any requests?" Dad asked as we settled in the car.

"All I want right now is a home-cooked meal." I replied.

"No problem. But first we have to stop by Grams's. She wants to see you before anyone."

We pulled out into the traffic and for the most part enjoyed the ride in silence. My family and I didn't talk a whole lot in the car because we liked to listen to music and think. It was good to be with them freely, with no time limit. I feel like I was back in the world.

However, the conversation here and there helped pass the time. We eventually pulled up to Grams's. She waited for us on the steps of her house. When Dad stopped the car, I jumped out and ran into her arms. All I could do was cry. Grams meant everything to me. It felt so good to smell her fragrance.

When we went inside the house, a chorus of voices shouted, "Surprise!" My family was all there; some had even flown in from Europe, Trinidad, Italy, DC, the Dominican Republic, San Francisco, and Hawaii. It was beyond belief. I hadn't seen some of them in years. I couldn't stop the tears from rolling down my face.

We all chatted while smelling the aroma of the home-cooked meal in the kitchen. I happened to look over my shoulder and saw my best friend Teza was there pregnant with her and my brother Ohaji's first child. I quickly ran over to her. No one had told me. They wanted it to be a surprise, but I was a little hurt. I'd missed so much of my family and friends lives because of the decisions I'd made. I felt like I had missed out on a lot.

I then spotted Shaun out of the corner of my eye, sitting on the couch with his son Justin in his arms. My heart dropped to my stomach, and I froze for a short period. Justin was absolutely adorable. He would've been even cuter if I'd been the momma, I thought. His mother didn't seem to be present as Grams walked into the living room to announce that the food was ready. We all gathered as my dad led us in prayer. I looked around as he spoke, taking in every face and every moment. I couldn't believe this was happening. I took in every moment. I was hopeful of what God could do. I'd just always imagined I would be stuck in that cage forever. The two and a half years there had seemed like forever, like eternity.

We all ate and drank while I caught up on what was going on in everyone's lives new boyfriends, girlfriends, husbands, careers, and everything in between. After a few hours the party wound down and started to get smaller and smaller, until those who were left started cleaning up. While packing food in the kitchen, I stared out the backdoor window and daydreamed. I had a lot to do in order to catch up with everyone else. I felt so behind.

Snapping back to reality, I found Shaun standing quietly behind me.

"So what's the plan now?" he asked.

"What plan? I have so many." I replied.

"I'm talking about for us."

I looked at him as if I had seen a ghost. "I guess we could be friends. But you seem to have moved on with your life. I don't want to keep you from that." I sat down on a stool at the kitchen bar.

He hesitated, hanging his head down a bit. "Justin's mother is no longer alive. I'm raising him by myself."

The words echoed through my mind. "Sorry to hear that. You never said anything. What happened?" I tried to sound as if I cared.

"She died giving birth to Justin. The doctors told her it was a risk, but she was willing to take it." He sat down too.

"She was stubborn, and unselfish. I respect that." I meant that, but I was ready to end this conversation.

"We were never together. She was just a one-night stand and the condom broke. I couldn't walk away."

"Typical," I said under my breath.

"What?"

"Nothing." I got up and started to walk away, but he grabbed my wrist.

"Dila, I would love for us to start over and get back together. Let's see how things work out."

"Shaun, it's been two years. People change. You may not even like me anymore."

"So what, are you saying you don't love me anymore?"

"I'm just saying people change." I pulled away from him and bent to pick up a cup off the floor, trying my hardest not to look at him.

"We haven't changed that much," he said. "It's worth a try."

Silence quickly stole the moment.

Chapter 10

I made the decision to give Shaun another chance, and I didn't regret it. My first six months out of jail were blissful. I was in love, and I loved being a stepmom to Justin. Though I'd never thought about having a kid at twenty-five, I enjoyed him more than I ever could have expected. He was crawling and walking. It was exciting to see this little person growing.

The only problem I had with the kid thing is all the crying when I'm trying to get some sleep. I mean come on, who invented these elements? (Don't answer that question, please.) I also chose to move back in with Shaun. If it was a bad move I would eventually find out. For the time being, it worked; it felt like we'd never parted ways. I was a full-time, stay-at-home mom, which was just as much work as any job would be. I enjoyed it, but I felt like I was wasting my days away. I thought about going back to school to get a law degree. The only catch was I would have to let the school know I was a convicted felon, and that could prevent me from being accepted.

Regardless, I figured applying wouldn't hurt. I had more to gain than lose. And I was sure it would all fall into place as it always did.

As usual, when I needed guidance, I called Grams. She knew what to do.

"Grams, how are you?' I asked, excited to hear her voice.

"I'm good, baby. Cleaning," Grams said, taking a deep breath.

"Grams, I'm calling you because I want to get your thoughts on me going back to school for a law degree. The only thing is I don't think anyone would accept me because I was in prison."

"Well, you never know what's possible until you put yourself out there and see what happens," she told me. "God works in amazing ways, and you'd be surprised by the things he can work out. You know what? It's been a while but one of my old students I talk to from time to time works as an admissions counselor at Harvard Law School." Grams was a retired high school guidance counselor and she knows a lot of people. "I'll see what I can do. How's that sound?"

"Grams, you are the freaking best!"

"Just give me all of the information the school will need and I'll get it into the right hands."

"I'll drop everything off when I come from the grocery store tomorrow morning, if that's okay." I suddenly felt invincible. "Thanks, Grams."

"Anytime. I'm here for you in any way you need me. I'll talk to you later. Love you."

"I love you too."

I hung up the phone ecstatic with possibilities. The rest of that evening I could hardly think of anything else. I spent the whole night doing the application I reused my undergrad essay with a few changes, typed up my own recommendations, and planned to have my previous boss from the grocery store and my college basketball coach sign them in the morning. I would also pick up my transcripts when I visited my college coach. I was so excited, I didn't sleep a bit.

The next morning Justin and I went to the grocery store. I hardly recognized the place—it had been remodeled in the two years since I'd seen it. I put Justin into the buggy and found the nearest employee.

"Excuse me is Mr. Thomas here?" I asked one of the workers.

"Yes, he is. I'll page him for you." As the worker sent an intercom page for Mr. Thomas, I wrote out a small list of items to purchase.

"Phadila!" I heard a familiar voice behind me.

"Mr. Thomas, how are you?" I reached out to him for a hug.

"How are you? What are you doing here?"

"I'm good. I've come by to see if you'll sign this recommendation for me for graduate school." I handed it to him and he scanned the paper as I spoke. "I've been out of prison for about six months and I really want to take my chance at law school."

Mr. Thomas smiled. "You know I'll recommend you for anything. You were one of my best employees. Where do you need me to sign?"

"Right here. I made two copies just in case I apply somewhere else. Thank you so much."

I then headed to my old college St. John's University, "Excuse me. I want to order two official transcripts," I told the lady in blue across the counter.

"That'll be five dollars apiece," she replied.

"I need to get them right now if possible. Will that still be five dollars?"

"Yes. I can do it for you right now. Can I have your name and Social?" I gave her the money and information she asked for, and I waited less than five minutes for her to return with the transcripts.

"Thank you so much. I really appreciate it. You have a blessed day," I said, carrying Justin on my hip as I walked out the office door.

Justin and I left and headed to Gram's house. She was in the front of her brownstone, working on her flower garden. Her face lit up like Christmas lights as I opened the car door and made my way over to her.

To keep my mind off of the application, I took a part-time job as a night janitor at an elementary school, but it wasn't what I wanted to do with my life. I quit after a couple of months and tried to figure out my next move

First, I didn't want to believe prison had control over my life. I had options. I needed to work out things in case I didn't get into Harvard. I needed some solid plans, and I needed them fast.

I knew I could run a successful business—I had done it for years. It would just have to be something legal. I would probably have to work for someone else for a while, but I wanted to make my own schedule and have a say in what I did. And I'd have to work ten times harder than I ever had.

I made a commitment to myself and my life that morning, and I kept it in mind as the days passed. I posted them in my closet so I could see them every day but Shaun couldn't. His only plan for me was to be a housewife. Clearly he'd forgotten who he was dealing with.

* * *

I wasn't sure how I would get where I wanted to be, but I planned on figuring it all out soon.

"Who is it?" I asked, upset with whoever was banging at my front door after I'd gotten Justin to sleep.

"FedEx!" the baritone replied.

"Why are you knocking on my door like you're crazy?" I opened the door and stepped forward as if I were about to hit him. He asked me to sign for an envelope.

"Thank you," he said, then turned to walk back to his truck. I pulled my thoughts together and closed the front door. I then looked at the envelope in my hand. The return address said "Playboy." on the front. It was for Shaun, but since I wanted to be nosy, I opened it.

"You are invited to be a judge," the letter inside read. They were asking Shaun to be a judge for a model call they were having soon. Right then it hit me: I could be a Playboy model! I quickly read through the invitation for more details. I knew Shaun would feel some kind of way about me doing this type of modeling, but I had to make my way in the world. I called Phalana and Randy to tell them of my plan.

"Hi, guys" I said as they both picked up on the three-way call.

"What are you so excited about?" Randy asked.

"Right, what's up?" said Phalana.

"I decided I'm going to try out to be a Playboy model," I said, ready for whatever they were about to say.

"Phadila," Phalana said. "Are you serious? Have you talked to Shaun about this?"

"No. I will,"

"Phadila, you know he's not going to be okay with this," Randy interrupted. I knew he wouldn't be. Deep down inside I didn't care. I just hoped it would get me to where I wanted to be.

"I know, but it could help me get to a point where I can eventually start my own company," I said. "It would make things a little easier."

"Well, easier is one way to put it." I could practically hear Phalana rolling her eyes at me. "You'll forever be that naked girl, not that businesswoman you want to be."

I hadn't thought of it like that, but I wouldn't give in to their opinions. "It's so easy for you two to judge because you have things where you want them. I don't! No one's going to give me a chance. I'll never be more than a felon."

"I'm not judging, and stop using your prison time as an excuse," Randy said. "Gee whiz, I'm just shocked you'd be willing to do it. But hey, if you do, I'll support you. I am your friend."

She didn't sound very genuine, and neither did Phalana. "Dila, I don't think this is the way to do it, but like Randy said, I'll support you." They both sounded hesitant.

"Thanks, guys. But I'll do it with or without your approval."

"So why'd you even call us?" Phalana replied.

"Your only problem is going to be Shaun," Randy said.

"Yeah, I'm going to tell him. He'll be home in a few days, before the model call," I said.

"You're going to wait until days before? Not a good plan," my sister said. We all laughed.

"I agree," said Randy. "Besides, Phadila they don't have a lot of black girls in *Playboy*, so where are you going to fit in? If you go make sure you look better than the rest of the girls there."

"I will! I'll figure everything out."

I ended the phone call and sat on the couch to think. First I needed a workout plan just to tighten things up a bit. Randy was right—I was a girl of color, and *Playboy* usually only had one of us at a time. I had to walk in there looking better than every other chick.

Second, the model call was a week and a half away, so I had time to tell Shaun. He was traveling. I would save the news 'til he came home. I kept trying to tell myself he would be okay with it but even if he wasn't, it didn't matter. My mind was made up and nothing was going to change it.

From that day forward, I went running every morning, pushing Justin in his stroller. I would do about five miles, then come home do fifty push-ups and five hundred sit-ups. As much as I hated water, I drank a lot of it. I also pushed myself away from the table when I was done with a meal.

To my surprise, Shaun came home a few days early. He walked in on me doing sit-ups in the living room.

"Hey! What's up?" I asked, excited to see him but out of breath.

"What are you doing?"

"Sit-ups!" I finished my last one and got up to hug him. "How was your trip?"

"It was cool." He looked at me sideways, like I was a little crazy.

I took a sip of my bottled water and handed him the FedEx envelope. He sat down on the sofa to open it.

"So, I decided to find a less stressful and fun way to keep myself busy," I said. "It will also help me to start my own company eventually. I'm going to audition to be a Playmate."

He looked up from the invitation, his mouth in a frown. "You're out of your mind! Don't you know you have to be naked?"

"Yes, I know. I'm okay with that. I'm thinking about the long term. I've been working out to get my body on point."

He looked me up and down, grudgingly appreciating my work.

"They want you to be a judge," I continued, "and I figured if you are, then you could pick me. No one would know."

He threw the envelope on the table. "Dila, you've lost your damn mind. I'm not going to be a judge and if I were, I wouldn't pick you. You're not about to be photographed naked for everyone to see. I don't agree with your choice."

He got up and walked into the kitchen. I followed him, the envelope in my hand.

"Shaun, I really need something that can help me get to the next level. I'd be naked, yes! But it's done really classy. There aren't many options. I just want it to be a stepping-stone."

I wrapped my arms around his waist from behind and laid my head on his back.

"Dila, it's not happening. I don't approve. Keep looking. There's something else out there for you. He turned to hug me back. "What's wrong with being a Playmate?" I continued.

"Nothing. You just ain't doing it." Frustrated, I turned back toward the living room.

"It really won't be that bad," I replied, smiling ear to ear.

"You won't be doing it so of course it won't be!" I shot him a smirk and rolled my eyes. Clearly we were done with the conversation because he wasn't having it.

Chapter 11

"Hi," I said when I walked into the house. I dropped everything and went to the bedroom, to prepare for a shower.

My cell phone rang. "Hi mom," I said the minute I picked up the phone. "hi Love, what are you doing tomorrow? I wanna do a spa day." My mom got straight to the point. "I'm not doing anything. I would love to go to a spa. I need it so bad." I replied. "Good, let's say around noon. I'll call you in the morning." My mom knew how much I loved having spa days with her. "Okay, I'll be ready." I hung up the phone to notice the look on Shaun's face not being very happy. As if my phone call made him nervous. "What time are you leaving tomorrow? My mother and I are going to have a spa day together. I could not wait. I turned and went to the bathroom for my shower and prepared for dinner.

Over dinner, Shaun didn't say much. He seemed to be really annoyed. "Babe is everything okay?" I asked helping Justin with his cup.

"Yeah," he replied never looking up. "can I ask you something?" I asked curiously. He looked at me never saying yes or no. "What am I doing to make you so unhappy?" I replied to his look. "Phadila, why do you always want to go there with me? We're at the dinner table let's just eat for once. Dang, I get enough stress from my job. I don't need to come home to it." I didn't say a word I continued eating. I left it alone because I didn't want to upset him. The rest of the night I was anxious while Shaun seemed really annoyed. He hardly said two words to me.

The next morning he told me he'd decided not to leave until 5:00, which meant he could watch Justin while I went to the spa to have a little me time. I got ready, left to pick up my mom and we had a wonderful time A few hours after our mother daughter spa day I drove him to the airport. We were silent the entire way.

"I know I keep asking but are you not happy?" I asked as we pulled into the parking lot.

"Everything is cool. I'm happy," he replied.

"Then what's wrong?"

"Nothing much, Just focusing on the work I need to get done."

"You seem so distant. I just wanted to check." I turned off the car. He leaned over and kissed me on my cheek, then said goodbye. I sat there watching him as he entered the airport, then I drove off.

Chapter 12

I had been trying to figure out where I needed to start with my new life as a free woman that I hadn't noticed all the mail that had been sitting on the kitchen counter for days. As I scrimmaged through the pile I came across a big, white envelope from Harvard Law School's admissions office. My heart immediately skipped as I opened it.

"Congratulations, Phadila Lombardijones, you have been accepted into Harvard University Law School," read the letter inside. I gasped for air, tears rolling down my face. I reread it several times to make sure I hadn't read it wrong. I praised God! Then I called Grams to tell her the news.

"Grams, thank you, thank you so much! You just don't understand how much this means to me."

"What did I do?" she asked.

"I was accepted into Harvard Law School!"

She paused. "Congrats. I'm proud of you. But I'm not who you need to be thanking. You should thank God. He made it all possible."

"I already did. And I promise I won't take this opportunity for granted. I'll make you and God and everyone else proud."

"You've already made us proud. You took a chance on yourself."

For the rest of the night I looked through the paperwork, but before long I put it all aside. I knew I wanted to stay off campus because Justin would be with me, God willing. I wanted to rent a townhouse close to the school. I also didn't pay much attention to the financial aid papers. I was going to pay my tuition in full.

Eventually I finished filling out all the paperwork and decided I would take a week or two off to go to Cambridge. Too excited to sleep, I had to tell someone else, so I called my dad, who was already half sleep.

"Hi Daddy," I was too excited to care about waking him.

"Hi, love. How are you?" he asked.

"You'll never guess what I'm about to say."

"I don't know. What?" Dad didn't seem to be in a figuring out mood.

"I got accepted into Harvard Law School!" I said, smiling from ear to ear.

"Get out of here, for real?" He woke up my mom to let her know too.

"Yes! I got the letter today."

"That's great, Phadila! I'm proud of you. Congrats!"

"I think I'm going to go to Cambridge to look for an apartment soon."

"That would be good. I'll go with you to help out. If that's what you would like." Dad was very good at real estate stuff.

"Yes. Thanks, Daddy. You're the best. Well, I'll let you get back to sleep. Tell mom I love her too."

After we finished talking I spent the rest of the night trying to figure out my game plan. I wasn't sure how things would work out. Justin was old enough for daycare. As for Shaun, he would need to get in where he fit in. He was usually gone so much he'd probably hardly be around anyway. I'm sure he won't be happy about my plan to reside in Cambridge until school is done, but we could discuss it when he's home. I did want to share the news with him too so I decided to call.

Even though I knew he wouldn't be excited about my big accomplishment, I decided to call and tell him about it anyway.

"Hey," I said as he answered. "Babe, I got accepted into Harvard!"

He remained quiet. "That's good for you. Congrats."

"Thanks. Are you busy?"

"Nah, everything is cool. I'm going to have to call you back though."

"No!" I replied. "I'm trying to talk to you. It's been days."

He was quiet for a moment. "Dila, I got a lot to do right now. You're alive and well, and that's all I need to know. We can talk about everything when I come home."

As I started to respond, all I heard was a dial tone. I tried calling back several times but he didn't answer. Something was wrong. But tonight I wouldn't let anything or anyone steal my joy.

* * *

At 6 a.m. I was still awake. I quickly rounded up everything I needed to call a moving company and have dad call a real estate agent so maybe we could move things that weekend. It was June, and I figured it would be good to get settled in before school started in August. I could feel the city out a bit and maybe take a couple of pre-courses.

Justin woke up in the midst of my excitement to go potty. Not long after he fell back to sleep and before I could realize it was 10 a.m.. As I began to cook breakfast my dad called, saying he had worked some things out for me. He found a real estate agent who found a really nice townhouse. He emailed me pictures of the place and it was beautiful.

A week later I hired movers to help with the move to Cambridge and booked plane tickets for the following week. Everything was moving so fast, I had no time to think about it, or about Shaun's strange behavior. He never called me back to smooth things over. on Friday I sat on the flight next to my mom nearly in tears. I couldn't prove anything was wrong with Shaun, but deep down I knew something wasn't right.

"Dila, don't worry yourself," Mom said. "Everything will work out."

I looked up from the magazine in my lap. "I know. It's just that he hasn't called." I could feel the emotion balling up in my throat, and I didn't want to cry. The tears fell anyway. I wiped them away quickly.

"He will be where he wants to be. You can't make anything what it's not."

"How did you know I was thinking about Shaun?" I asked.

"I'm your mother. It doesn't take much to figure out when a man is the problem." She smiled and went back to reading her book. I glanced over at Justin as he slept, wondering how things would play out for his sake. I sat quietly, looking at the pictures in my magazine and appreciating how my mom never pressed an issue. She'd said what she felt was needed and moved on. I always appreciated that about her.

When the plane landed, I woke Justin up and we disembarked. Every step I took was full of anticipation and excitement. We made our way through the airport, met up with the driver, and we were in route to our new home.

Just as we pulled away, my phone rang. It was Shaun.

"Hi, babe," I answered. "I miss you. Where are you?" I was still upset about not hearing from him, but at least he hadn't forgot about me completely.

"I'm good," he whispered. "You called me?"

"Yes, days ago, So you don't miss me too?"

My mom softly tapped my wrist, signaling for me to let him say the words without help.

"Yeah, yeah I do. I've just been very busy." I heard voices in the background.

"Why are you whispering?" I asked him. "And why can't you just say you miss me too?"

"What are you tripping about? I've just been busy. I didn't forget about you, homey!"

My face went blank. *Homey*? He'd never called me that.

"I'll call you when I get out of the studio," he said, then the call disconnected.

Chapter 13

Our new townhome was small, but it was enough room for the three of us. Not that Shaun would ever be there; I hadn't spoken to him since the day I'd arrived in Cambridge. Surprisingly I hadn't thought about him much either.

I got Justin into daycare and I went to school to register for a couple of summer classes. I met a really cool chick there named Sheena, who was originally from Alabama. We clicked really well and her shoe game was so on point!

Monday morning I was up bright and early for my first class. I dropped Justin off early at daycare so I could have a moment to relax. As I got myself together, my cell phone rang.

"Hello," said a woman. I didn't recognize her voice. "I'd prefer not to give my name, but I want to talk to you about Shaun."

"Okay." I took a deep breath, sat down at the kitchen bar, and got ready to take in whatever she had to tell me.

"Well, I don't want you to take this the wrong way, and if you need evidence I can surely get you some. I don't know if you know, but Shaun's been in a relationship with my best friend Kimmie for going on three years now."

My heart dropped, and my entire body went numb. "How did they meet?" I felt so stupid asking.

"They met at a video shoot and have been together ever since. I told her long ago that I'd heard he has a girlfriend and child, but she didn't believe me. Nor did she seem to care. I'm coming to you woman to woman because if I were ever in the same situation, I hope someone would tell me." She paused. "They're walking into the room right now, so I have to hang up."

I had so many questions I wanted to ask, but I didn't have the chance. I argued in my head on whether or not I should believe. I didn't want to assume this woman was lying because I'd already had a feeling something was going on.

Besides, she didn't know me from a can of paint, why would she lie?

I was torn, but I had to pull it together because I had a class to go to. I got everything I needed and went on my way. In class I couldn't focus one bit. I sent a text message to Shaun, telling him to call me when he got the time.

Every now and then, a fireball of tears would emerge in my throat and I would try to stop it. I felt so betrayed, dumb, and used. Here I was playing house with someone who was playing house with someone else.

After that class was over, I drove to the closest liquor store, then went back to the school parking lot. Two shots turned into a pint of gin. I cried until my eyes were bloodshot red and I was late for my next class. As I stumbled in, Shaun texted me back.

"What's up?" he wrote.

"Nothing much," I typed back. "You haven't called. I was just checking on you. Have you been that busy?"

"Nah. I'll be in Cambridge tomorrow. I wanted it to be a surprise."

I didn't reply. I simply put my cell in my purse and sat at my desk.

"Oh damn, Dila," Sheena said, sitting down next to me. "Girl, you need a whole bag of peppermints. You smell like straight liquor." She said laughing a little and handing me a pack of gum from her bag.

I still didn't say a word. I wanted to burst into tears.

"Honey, whatever it is, it can't be so bad that you're willing to smell like an alleyway."

I laughed, trying to block everything out of my mind.

"We'll talk after class," Sheena whispered as the professor began to give his lecture.

During class some of everything went through my mind. I caught Sheena glancing at me several times to make sure I was okay. When class ended she took me to a nearby pub to sit and talk.

"So what's so bad that you had to drink a whole bottle before class?" she asked as I sipped a glass of water.

"I feel so stupid," I said, looking out the window, afraid to see her expression.

"Phadila, what happened?"

I looked at her. "I got a phone call from some girl who told me Shaun has been in a whole other relationship for the past three years." I took another sip of my water, hoping it would slow down my tears.

Sheena froze. "Do you believe it? Have you spoken to him about it?"

"I don't know what to believe. All of the signs say it's true. But my heart just doesn't want to believe he would stoop that low to be in another relationship while still with me? I don't want to believe it."

"Sleeping with a woman and being in a relationship with a woman are two different things, at least to men."

"I know, but he's been acting really funny lately. He hardly even calls to check on his own son. When we talk he's in a rush or has an attitude. And he called me *homey*." I sat back in my seat.

"Wow." Sheena raised her eyebrows and sipped her drink. "I don't know Shaun, but maybe he's stressed. He's in a business where women throw themselves at him. This woman who called doesn't know you. For all you know she could be trying to break y'all up. With that being said, people are not what they say or think. They are what they do. So if Shaun's actions are funny, maybe something's up. Again, I don't know him. It's just my small observation."

I sigh looking out the restaurant window. "You're right. He claims he'll be here tomorrow. So we'll see." I smiled at her. "Thanks, Sheena. I really appreciate you listening. I was ready to go bombs over Baghdad."

"I will say this." Sheena waved a waitress over to order some food. "Just pray about it and give it to God. He'll make everything show its face, whether it's good or it's bad."

We paid for our meals walking out of the pub hand in hand, as best friends sometimes do. We said our goodbyes and went our separate ways. I quickly rushed to pick up Justin, while praying as Sheena suggested: "Lord, I'm unsure where I am in my life right now. You've given me everything I've dreamed of and hoped for. Yet I'm still unhappy. Lord, I don't want to idolize anyone but you, and I feel like I'm putting my relationship on a pedestal that even you may not reach. Lord, if this situation is mine, please give me the strength to handle it with my head held high, the wisdom to understand it all, and the courage to stand up for what I know I deserve. Lord, you are all. You see all. And I will always give my all to you first and foremost. In Jesus's name I ask and pray. Amen!"

Chapter 14

I picked Shaun up at the airport the next morning.

"Hey, momma," he said as he walked up to the passenger side of the car. I smiled, but I didn't budge to help him with his bags or to embrace him. He got in and leaned over to kiss my cheek, then we rode all the way to the house in silence. When we got there he got Justin out of the car as I pulled his smallest bag from the trunk.

"Babe, just leave those. I'll get them," he said continuing, "Which way it was to Justin's bedroom?" I let him put Justin to sleep and I went back to bed myself. I woke up a few hours later to find Shaun asleep on the living room sofa. I left him there and headed out to class.

Afterward I met up with Sheena at the pub again.

"Shaun's home," I said stuffing my mouth with a double cheeseburger.

"So have you talked about the phone call you got?"

"Nah. We haven't said a word to each other. He probably knows something is up."

"Well, he won't know for sure until you say something." Sheena ate some of my French fries and stared off across the bar. "I met a guy yesterday in the grocery store. He's so cute. He seems really nice."

"That's good. I'm happy for you. What's his name?"

"Jason, we're going out on a date tomorrow and I am excited."

I gave her a high-five. "Yes! Just don't be as dumb as I've been."

"Girl, shut up!" Sheena laughed.

When I got home that evening, Shaun was in the kitchen, talking on the phone. I set my car keys on the counter and took off my shoes, then told Justin to go to play in his room. Shaun quickly hung up the phone.

"Who was that?" I asked.

"It was my mom. What's up? Where have you two been?"

"Really? I've never seen you that happy to talk to her."

I finished getting comfortable and grabbed a bottle of water out of the refrigerator noticing that Shaun watched my every move. He went into the living room and sat on the sofa. I sat next to him but he moved over as if he didn't want sit next to me. I acted like I didn't notice and assumed he was giving me some space. After a while I got up to clean the house, and Shaun got into the shower. Still trying to see what's going on I attempted to get in with him.

"What are you doing?" he asked.

"We used to always take showers together," I said.

"I'm trying to relax. I want to shower by myself. Please get out!" He shoved me back a little.

I kissed his chest. "I can relax you."

His body grew tense. "Phadila, please." I knew he was annoyed, but I continued.

"Why don't you want to touch me?" I asked.

"I didn't say that! I just want to be alone. I got somewhere to be and I want to get my mind right before I get there." He turned away from me as if hiding his body, as if it were my first time seeing him.

"You don't know anyone here," I said. "Where do you have to be?"

"You don't know who I know."

"Are you talking about Kimmie?" I asked as I picked up my clothes and wrapped a towel around me. He quickly rushed to close the shower curtain and I went into the bedroom. I waited for him to get out so I could finish my shower. We use to shower together all the time.

I finished and got settled for bed. Still a bit unsure, I tucked Justin into bed and I went into my room to read a few more chapters for class. After reading I watched a little TV, double checked that the front door was locked. As

I passed through the living room, Shaun hadn't move from the sofa since the last time I'd come through.

"Are you coming to bed?" I asked, already assuming the answer to the question was no.

"Nah, I'm about to leave in a second, but I'll probably sleep on the couch again." he said, not even looking up at me to catch my reaction.

I smirked. "Okay." I bent down to give him a kiss. He moved out of the way and put his hand up to block my lips. I switched my hip to the left and placed my hand on it.

"So what's really the problem?" I asked, angry. He sat there like I hadn't said a word. "So who the hell is Kimmie?"

He sat the remote on the table and looked up at me.

"You know, your girlfriend of what? Three years now?" I asked.

"I don't know who Kimmie is. I'm just tired and I haven't been in the mood for anything." He sat back and put his foot on the coffee table. I quickly hit it down.

"So tired that you don't want to touch me? Am I that bad now? Or is she just that good?" I sat down on the table, leaving him no choice but to face me.

"Dila, again, I just have a lot on my mind. And I don't know a Kimmie." He folded his arms and just looked at me. As much as I didn't want to believe him, I did.

"Look me in my face and tell me you don't have a girlfriend!" I said.

He moved closer until our noses nearly touched. "There's no one else but you, Dila." He kissed my forehead, trying to ease the conversation. "Shaun there has to be someone else. Your actions would only then make sense." I replied leaning back into the couch. "Phadila, why do we have to do this? Really, why can't you just listen to what I'm saying and stop assuming that I'm lying?" he replied leaning towards me. "Shaun because I know you are lying. I know! I can't put a finger on it but I know." I began to cry, "We have been together for a long time and I love you so much. I don't deserve whatever it is that you are doing to me. There are plenty of men I know who would love a woman like me. Why can't you love me like I love you?" I could sense the anger in his face as he stood up replying," what the hell are you talking about other men? Is this what this conversation is about? You want someone else? Well it isn't happening!" I also stood to my feet, "No, this isn't about me wanting someone else. This is about you being with me and loving me not everyone else. This is about how much you've change, our relationship has changed. You don't care and it hurts because I thought we we're planning our life together as a family? I thought it was forever?" Shaun didn't know what to say as he simply replied. "Okay Phadila let's just go to bed because we're never going to get to the end of this."

Sadly I did just that. I knew we would have this same argument again because we keep having it. I just have so much love for what we have I want him to see how much he should love me.

Chapter 15

"What's going on?" I looked over at my alarm clock. It was 4:00 in the morning and Shaun was falling into bed. He was completely drunk and reeked of sex. "Shaun, what the hell? Where have you been?"

"Dila, leave me alone, please."

"Ugh. You smell like alcohol and ass!"

"Oh!" He rolled over and fell off the bed.

"Shaun, are you okay?"

He seemed to have passed out on the floor. I dragged him to the bathroom, undressed him, and put him in the tub in some cold water. He didn't budge. I sat up with him all night.

The next morning I gave him two Tylenols and headed to class. I couldn't believe how he was treating me as if it disgusted him just to be in my presence. How did we get to this point? What did I do? All I wanted to do was make things better. I didn't want to lose him. But I was fighting alone. I had been for a while.

For the next three days while Shaun was in town we hardly spoke. He went out to party all night and I stayed up worrying about him. On Thursday morning he caught a cab to the airport before I woke up.

I sent him a text message: "Have a nice trip." He never replied.

I continued to turn a blind eye to his disrespect. Honestly, I sometimes lived for the days when he was gone because everything was easier to manage emotionally. Though I wasn't as strong as I appeared to be, I was weak for him. I felt like I needed him as I went back and forth I could not lose him. It's obvious things are over? Shaun was no longer in love with me. I had to get it through my head. I mean something had to make it all click.

I decided to make it my business to find out about his other relationships. I knew snooping would be easy because he would never expect me to do it. I checked every bank statement to see where our money was going.

Didn't take much to find out he had another account with a woman's name on it: Kimberly McFar.

Stupid! I thought as I flipped through the paperwork. It was all there: her Social Security number, address, birthday everything I needed to know. I looked through all the paperwork he kept in his home office. The more I searched, the more I learned. Apparently they had spent our anniversary together at dinner. They also shared a condo here in Cambridge. I read through his phone's text messages online and found several cute little Post-it notes saying "I love you" and "I miss you." After a while I grew angry because he wasn't even smart enough to hide the proof any better.

As if he knew I was up to something, Shaun began to call me more often. I kept our conversations to a minimum; I needed to detach myself emotionally from the situation. The fourteen years we'd spent together was becoming a blur. I cried so much. I was hurt and disgusted with him. He would be home in a few more days left on his tour, I pulled together the things I needed to part ways as I got dinner ready.

I called Randy and told her about my decision. She was shocked. I called Phalana too. She tried to talk me out of it. But my mind was made up. I packed Shaun's belongings, called a moving company, and had them deliver it all to the condo he shared with his girlfriend. I split up all our joint accounts. Then I sent some flowers to Kimmie. "How you got him is how you'll lose him," the card read. I figured that said it all. When Shaun came home, his key would not open the door. He knocked until I let him in. He kissed me on my cheek and opened the refrigerator to get a glass of orange juice.

"What's going on with that door?" he asked. I watched him drink his juice.

"I got the locks changed," I told him.

"Why would you do that? Did someone try to break in?"

I rolled my eyes, irritated. "No. It's because you no longer live here. Surprise! You're moving out."

He looked confused.

"Remember when I asked you about Kimmie?"

He rolled his eyes at me. "Are you kidding? You're still on that? I told you."

"No, you didn't. You lied to my face. I went through all your stuff. Kimmie McFar, right?" I smiled at his blank expression. "Yeah, I know. I know where you two live, her Social Security number, her phone number, everything."

He took a step toward me. "Why are you going through my stuff?"

"That's all you have to say? Shaun, we've been together for almost fourteen years. I've given you everything while you're out there with women who aren't even half of me."

"What do you want me to say?"

"'I'm sorry' would help. Or maybe 'I messed up.'" I shook my head. "I want nothing more to do with you." My stomach was full of butterflies, but it felt so good to say all this to him.

"Phadila, honestly, Kimmie was just something to do. I want you. I've always wanted you. But you wanted to have a career. I just wanted you to be my woman, to be there when I wanted you, to enjoy the money I make. And that wasn't enough. Kimmie's okay with all that. I've always felt like you're never satisfied with what I give you."

"Are you kidding me? You were mad because I wanted to have a life of my own? You don't want me to have a mind of my own. If that's enough reason to go and be with someone else, you've got to be the dumbest fool on earth. You didn't have enough respect for me to say you didn't want to be with me anymore. You're a coward! Shaun I loved every bit of you good and bad. But I'm tired, I can't do this anymore. We can't keep doing this anymore." "Well, what do you want from me Phadila? I'm a man,   things happen. Does it really matter? I come home to you, no one else."

He said angrily "Are you kidding me? You come home to me but what do you do when you get here? Act like I don't even exist." As I replied something in me just knew it was over because I didn't have any more fight in me. "So I can't hang out with friends Phadila You want me to sit up in the house with you all day and do what?... Look at each other? I'm bored. You know how many women would love to be with me who would do everything in their power to keep me entertained? Do you?" I could not believe he played that card as I replied. "No I don't and I don't too much care. If you were bored all you had to do was open your mouth and tell me. How am I suppose know? Huh? I've been bending my back to make you love me and you still don't appreciate anything." I replied. "I never said I didn't love you. I damn sure don't love the girls I mess with from time to time. They are just something to do. I love you Phadila." For once he seemed genuine in his response but for once I wasn't trying to hear it anymore. "Just leave Shaun…Just leave please." I replied with my arms folded in disgust.

Justin came running into the kitchen. I gave him a huge hug, I was shattered. I had given him up so easily as if he meant nothing to me and he meant everything. Everything I'd built up until that point flashed before my eyes. I couldn't do anything but fall to the floor in tears. There was nothing I needed more than to hear my grandma's voice.

Chapter 16

The next morning I woke up with a knot in my throat and a huge headache from all the crying I did. I knew there was only one person I could call that could help me make sense of everything.

"Grams. How are you?"

"I'm good, honey. How are you?"

I didn't know how to reply because I wasn't sure how I was feeling. "I'm alive."

"You're better than alive. What's going on?"

"Grams, Shaun and I broke up for good this time." My voice trembled and I almost began to cry. "I couldn't take it anymore. He had to go."

"I understand. But you'll be okay. Things will work out as they should. You keep praying and being faithful to God. I promise you He will not fail you. No relationship is perfect. But that doesn't mean that you should limit your love either."

Grams continued,

"We all look to the people around us to show us how to love. But sometimes you got to learn from your own situation. Saving face for the kids works and sometimes it doesn't. Sometimes relationships work out and sometimes they don't. Justin is the innocent one in this situation and how he feels or how he'll take the breakup will say more about you and Shaun more than anything."

"You're right, Grams. But he needs me. I'm the only mother he's known." I sighed. I was heartbroken. "I'm sure it's too late to fight for custody"

"It's never too late, especially when a child is involved. But in this case I think maybe you should lay off for a while simply because of the toxic emotions between you and Shaun. And even though you're the only mother he's known. You are not his mother. I know how much you love Shaun and how much you want him to love you back but relax honey. Let this situation play itself out and if it's meant to be, it'll happen again."

"Grams, I swear you know everything," I said with a laugh.

"I'm nearly ninety years old. I better know something."

We both laughed.

"Grams, I'll let you go. Just wanted to update you and check in." I said, feeling happier than I had been in a while.

"Of course, love. Have a good day. I love you." Grams always knew how to put things into prospective. At least I felt like she did.

Grams's conversation stuck with me. I was still sad about not fully thinking out a better plan for Justin.

Months went by, and I entertained several guys just as friends, or as one night stands. Nothing ever stuck because I wasn't looking for anything. Honestly I didn't know what I was looking for. I didn't do much outside of school and the days just rolled on, each one the same as the last.

One dull and wet Saturday morning in October, I woke up and decided to go for a jog to clear my head. I turned on my iPod and hit the street, and by the two-mile mark I felt a little better. I also noticed someone familiar running nearby.

"Chris?" I asked. Chris Morris and I had gone to grade school together in Brooklyn. When we got older I'd always had a bit of a crush on him, but he and Shaun had never gotten along. We've never hung out, but we always passed each other in the neighborhood.

"Phadila Lombardijones," he said, stopping and giving me the biggest smile. He reached in for a hug.

"How are you? What are you doing in Cambridge?" I asked.

"I'm good. I've been here for work for about three years. I do marketing for a local nonprofit." He said as he looking me up and down typical man. "I should be asking you what you're doing here."

"I'm here for school. I go to Harvard Law."
I scoped him out as well.

"Wait, you go to Harvard? Wow, you got out
of prison and made it happen. I see you still got
it!"

"I'm trying."

"You're way beyond trying, trust me. So are
you here by yourself? Where's Shaun?" he asked,
looking around.

"I'm alone. Shaun and I broke up a few
months ago." It still felt funny to say it out
loud.

"Well, that's too bad. Maybe I can finally
take you out on a date or hang out with you."

I smiled. "I see nothing wrong with that."

We exchanged numbers and I got back to my
jogging. I turned to look behind me and he was
still standing there watching me run away. By the
time I got home, he had already left me a
voicemail.

"Hi, Phadila. It was nice seeing you earlier. If you're not busy, please let me treat you to dinner tonight. Call me back."

I jumped into the shower, laid out something to wear and returned his call.

"I see you waste no time," I said when he answered.

"I can't let a great opportunity pass me by."

I smiled at his comment. "Dinner sounds good tonight. I have a taste for seafood."

"Sounds good to me, text me your address and I'll be there in a few."

Twenty minutes later Chris pulled up in the driveway and we were on our way out, "You went all out," I told him as he pulled out a chair for me at the table. "You didn't have to."

"Yes I did. I've been infatuated with you since we were kids. It's only right for me to treat you as good I feel about you."

I blushed as he continued. "Infatuated is good. I'm pretty sure once I get to know you a little better we may be in love."

The waiter brought over a bottle of red wine.

"We'll see," I replied. "I'm not really looking, but I'm open to anything that's worth my time."

I took a sip of the wine he poured into my glass, picked up my menu off the table, and ordered.

"I'll have the smoked salmon with steamed broccoli and asparagus." The waiter nodded his head and turned to walk back toward the kitchen. Chris took a sip of wine, looking at me over the top of the glass.

"So you're single? I thought Shaun would never let you go."

"Yeah, well, sometimes things happen and life still goes on."

"May I ask why you broke up?"

"Infidelity." I paused. I didn't really want to go there. "Let's talk about you. Why are you single? You seem like a great guy."

"Well, that's a good question that I don't have an answer for. I've been so into my work, I haven't had time for anything else. I haven't even been out to enjoy the city." He swooshed the wine around in his glass.

"Sounds boring," I replied. We both laughed.

"Yeah, it has been. But I love what I do. I wouldn't trade it for anything in the world."

The waiter brought our meals ten minutes later. We ate, drank, and enjoyed great conversation. He dropped me off at home and drove off into the night."Better than I expected." I said walking into my front door while waving goodnight to Chris.

Chapter 17

Six months into our friendship Chris made it clear to me that he wanted more. He wanted to make our relationship official, and I happily said yes. Before I realized it time had flown by and we were celebrating our one-year anniversary.

As time went on Chris ended up moving in with me. Things moved very quickly, but we were happily in love.

I continued on with school and work, so much that I didn't see Sheena as much. She had a new boyfriend and when she had time I was way too busy. I put my all into making Chris happy that I often neglected myself and my own needs. I found myself falling into the same trap I'd got stuck in with Shaun. I spent nights crying and begging God to make whatever it was that I was going through better.

"Baby, is everything okay?" Chris rolled over late one night to comfort me.

"I just have a lot on my mind." I replied, trying to hide my tears.

"Are you sure?"

"Yeah." I got up to go to the bathroom and stayed in there for almost an hour. Chris went back to sleep. The next morning I went on my usual jog and made a needed call to Grams.

"Hi, Grams." I said as she picked up.

"Hi, baby. How are you? I miss you, sweetie."

Emotion started to fire up in my chest. "I miss you, Grams so much. Something is wrong and I don't know what it is."

"Did something happen?"

"I don't know. Everything is great. I have school, work, and a good man, but I feel like something is missing." Tears began to run down my face.

"Dila, you need to sit down and figure out what's wrong. You have to learn how to evaluate your feelings so you don't end up bitter for no reason."

I sat down on a bench. I couldn't run anymore. "Grams, honestly, I think I know what it is. I think I'm still in love with Shaun." My body felt a little different once I got that off my chest.

"Dila, you have to realize that sometimes things are not meant to be. If you and Shaun are, it'll happen. Until then you need to enjoy every good moment you are blessed to have because they may never happen again."

"I'm trying." I sniffled and wiped away my tears. "I promise I am. I know I should be over Shaun. He was doing wrong. But I feel like I'm overcompensating with Chris because deep down I feel like the breakup was my fault." I put my head down as people walked by seeming a little concerned.

"Phadila, do what you have to at this moment. You and Shaun will end up back together because years ago he promised me he would eventually marry you. I know for sure he still has that vision because I've spoken to him since you guys have gone your separate ways. He will realize he messed up. Things will fall into place."

Grams's statement shocked me. I sat quietly on the bench for some time.

"If you're so consumed with Shaun," she went on, "then you need to let Chris go because it will only lead to you hurting him or him hurting you. You need to be honest with yourself and with him."

Again she was right. But I didn't want to miss out on Chris. He had been a good man to me.

"Well, Grams, maybe it's just a feeling that I'm having right now. Maybe I'll shake it."

"Baby, when you're in love with someone, it's not shakable. You constantly find yourself looking over every little detail of the relationship and realizing what you could have done better or what you could have not done at all. That's part of being in love!"

She continued.

"Phadila, it's okay. We've all been there. We regret decisions we make, and sometimes decisions need to be made for us to get us where we need to be. In order for you and Shaun to come back together and be better for each other some things have to happen."

"Thanks, Grams. I know I can always count on you to break things down for me. "

"You know I'm here whenever you need me, Dila. Just call me."

I sat at the park a while longer, trying to clear my head. Chris called several times, and when I felt better I called him back.

"Hi, babe," I said. "I'm on my way home. I want to talk to you." I began jogging back to the house.

"Okay," he replied. He was in the kitchen when I walked into the house.

"Hey," he said as I took off my shoes. "You want to talk?"

"Yeah." I grabbed a bottle of water out of the cabinet and we sat down together at the dining room table.

"I don't really know what to say, where to start, or how to say any of it," I began. "However, I'm going to say it. I know you've noticed I've been crying myself to sleep a lot lately. Honestly I wasn't really sure why, but I think I have an idea."

I felt uncomfortable telling him this, and he looked uncomfortable preparing himself to hear what I was about to say.

"Okay, well what's going on?" he asked.

"I don't know a better way to say this besides I'm still in love with Shaun."

Chris became very stiff. He sat up straight and just looked at me.

"I love you, but I'm still in love with him," I went on. "He crosses my mind all the time. I feel like I could've fought harder for what we had. You're so good to me and I don't want to lose you. I just can't get past him."

"You mean to tell me we've been together all this time and you still can't get over your ex?" He was clearly upset.

"Yes! I know it's hard for you to understand, but you have to. I spent most of my life with this man. We built so much together, and I miss that."

"I can understand that, but what you have to understand is that man didn't treat you like you should have been treated. That man is probably not even thinking about you as much as you think about him. He wasn't even concerned when you two were together."

"I understand that. Please, Chris, I don't want to lose you. I just feel like sometimes I'm overcompensating with you for things I feel like I could've done in the past."

"Well, look. I'm here, and I don't plan on going anywhere. I'm in love with you and I'll stick around until you feel the same way. If you eventually say to me that you'll never be in love with me, then I'll deal with it then. But for now I'm willing to work through this."

"Chris, I love you. I swear I do, and I want to make this work. I just need a lot of work." I replied, laughing at myself.

"Time will heal old wounds." He got up and came around the table to hug me and kiss my cheek. "I will do my best to be better than the past. You deserve it," he whispered in my ear.

Slowly months rolled on, those old wounds did heal. Chris began to mean even more to me than ever before. Shaun still resurfaced in my head sometimes, but it was easier because I knew Chris understood. My sleepless, teary nights came to an end. Slowly I was able to get back to the old me.

* * *

To my surprise three months later I found out I was pregnant. I'd always wanted my own children, especially after losing Justin. To break the news to Chris, I decorated the living room with pink and blue bottles, balloons and even got some really cute cupcakes. I dang near ate them all before he made it home.

When he walked in from work and saw it everything he was in complete shock.

"Phadila! What's going on?"

I ran to him for a big hug. "Guess what?"

"You're giving someone a baby shower? Because I can leave."

I laughed. "No, silly. I'm pregnant."

Chris looked at all the decorations again. "You're what?"

"I'm pregnant!" I replied even more ecstatically than the first time.

"Um, we need to talk, Phadila." He didn't seem happy. "Maybe we should have talked about this before, but I don't want kids. You're going to have to get rid of.it."

My heart jumped to my throat. "You don't?" I was hardly able to get the words out.

"No, I don't!"

"Why are you just now telling me this? I want kids!" I began to tear up.

"I don't know. I'm sorry. But you're going to have to get an abortion."

I dropped my head into my hands and cried even harder. "I don't believe in abortion."

"Well either you have one or I'm out."

"I thought you said you loved me. You can't leave."

"This isn't about love, Phadila. It's about doing what's right, and right now is not the time for kids. It never will be, in my eyes."

I looked at him, trying to hold back my sobs. "Chris, you know this isn't right. You say you love me and you know I don't believe in aborting a baby." I replied no longer able to hold it all in. "Phadila, like I said I don't want any children. I do love you but we cannot do this right now. This isn't good for either of us. So either you get an abortion or you can have the baby but I will sign over my rights and have nothing to do with either of you." Chris was stern in his request. I didn't want to lose him and go back to being alone. So I replied, "I guess I can make an appointment to go in the morning. I'm not too far along." I got up and started taking down the decorations. "Chris, are you sure about this? I mean think of all the wonderful things this baby could bring us."

"Like what? Kids don't do anything but get in the way. I don't have time and neither do you. Phadila. I've never wanted kids. I don't want kids. Ever." He kicked his feet up on the coffee table and turned on ESPN as if the conversation never took place.

* * *

But I had to do it if I wanted to keep Chris happy. I picked up the phone called my gynecologist and made an appointment.

After I got off the phone I headed to work. I cried the whole way. When I arrived at my office I wiped my eyes with a cold rag in the ladies's restroom before heading upstairs. I figured it would make the redness and puffiness disappear.

"Hi, Faye," I said, walking quickly pass one of my coworkers with my head down.

"Hi, Dila, is everything okay?" she asked.

"Yeah, everything is good, just really tired." I tried to cover my eyes up with my hair. I went straight into my office and closed the door behind me, hoping I could seclude myself until the crying passed. The minute I sat down at my desk, Sheena called.

"Dila, what's going on?" she asked.

"Sheena!" I replied, the tears starting up again.

"Have you been crying? What's wrong?"

"Sheena, I really don't want to talk about it. I'm already ashamed and I haven't even done it yet." I said, turning my chair all the way around to look out the window.

"How in the world are you ashamed of thinking about something? We're grown-ass women. Man up and spill it."

I sat for a minute, looking at the floor, then replied. "I'm getting an abortion on

Thursday." Tears rolled down my face. It hurt so much to say it.

"You're *what*? Why?"

"Because I'm pregnant and Chris doesn't want to have any kids."

"Excuse me, but what happened to Phadila and what she wants? This isn't just Chris's child. It's yours too. And honestly, it's your body, so you have the last word."

I sat back in my chair. "I know the decision is mine, but I don't want to bring a child into a situation where it's not wanted. Anyway I have too much going on right now to stop and focus on a kid and I just don't want to lose him."

Sheena paused. "I'm sorry you have so much going on, but you should've thought about that when y'all were doin' the do unprotected. If Chris didn't want kids, why didn't he discuss it in the beginning of you guy's relationship. Besides, what he wants is irrelevant because it's your body that will be affected. If he decides he wants to leave, then let him! I don't know what gets into you when you start dating men. It's like you become so weak. I know your forever story is you want to be in love but this love thing that you're infatuated with is disgusting. Get it together, Phadila!

Chapter 18

My appointment for the abortion was on Thursday. That morning I still wasn't sure I had made the right choice. While getting ready to leave the house, I called Chris to see if he would come along for support.

"I don't want to be there," he said. "It's going to be so gross."

I was disappointed, to say the least. At least Sheena had already agreed to go along. I picked her up and we drove in silence, no music or talking. As I pulled up to the clinic and parked, she leaned over and took my hand.

"Dila, you don't have to do this."

I turned off the car. "I do." I took a deep breath. "I do."

Inside, the clinic smelled and looked clean beyond belief. I guess I'd assumed abortion clinics weren't clean or nice looking.

"Hi, I'm here for an appointment," I said through the glass window.

"Phadila LombardiJones?" the receptionist replied. She gave me paperwork to fill out and I took a seat next to the door, just in case I changed my mind at the last minute. I could hardly stop shaking long enough to fill out the paperwork.

"Why am I so nervous?" I asked Sheena.

"You're probably nervous because you shouldn't be doing this."

"Ms. Lombardijones," a voice called, I nervously rose from my seat. Sheena followed. We were escorted to a back room where I undressed and laid on a table. A doctor came in and explained what would take place, so after I was sedated. I don't remember a thing after that.

On the way out a nurse gave me a package of papers about things I was to do and not to do: check my temperature daily, take some meds, don't use tampons. To say I was in pain is an understatement. Everything hurt. Sheena drove me home and put me to bed. She also gave Chris some very choice words before she left.

"I can't stand Sheena sometimes," he said as he came into the bedroom. "She needs to learn to mind her business. Why did you even have to tell her?"

"She's my friend. And you didn't want to come. I needed support." A cramp shot through my abdomen, and I curled up in a ball.

"Do me a favor next time just keep our business between us." Chris stormed out of the bedroom like a child.

***

Within a day or two I felt better. And as the weeks rolled by, things with Chris settled down. Still, not a day went by that I didn't think about Justin, Shaun, or the abortion. About how I could have been a better girlfriend or how I could have worked things out. Shaun never would have asked me to get an abortion. But I did it to keep my man. I know he loves me and right now neither of us have time for a child.

I found myself falling into a small depression. I tried to focus on my schoolwork but I spent most of my time crying and regretting my decision. To keep my mind sane, I started to write in a journal. I wrote out my goals over and over in detail to start my own company. After classes I would talk to my professors about starting a law firm. A lot of them said it wasn't smart to do fresh out of school, but I was determined. I had it in my head, and I wanted to do it.

Academically I was on track. I had the second-highest grade point average in my class and was on my way to being valedictorian again. At home, Chris was a huge help at times, but then there were times he seemed to make even the simplest things harder. I just wanted Chris to be happy and to love me. As much as it kills me to think that I actually went through with the abortion, I know I did right by him and that's all that matters.

"I'm not doing anything this weekend. Are you still going to New York? I'll go with you."

That idea hadn't crossed my mind. I didn't see why he couldn't go, but honestly I just wanted to get away from him.

"If you want to," I replied, and left it at that. I got up and got ready for bed.

In New York I didn't see Chris much. He spent a lot of time with his family. Being there made me realize how much I missed being so close to mine too. Throughout my brief vacation I vowed to come back after graduation. I would talk to Chris about it, but either way I was coming home.

I called Chris to ask him to invite his family to my parent's for dinner. He didn't answer or return my call. My family and I had a wonderful dinner, but I felt so alone. Being home allowed a lot of things to play through my mind. To keep my head clear I decided to help my mom and I cleaned the kitchen.

"It always feels so much better when you come home," Mom said, leaning in for a hug. "You seem a little unhappy. Is everything okay?"

I sat down at the table. "I don't know where to start. I miss being home. Sheena has a new boyfriend who I think is too controlling, so I worry about her. Also, I didn't want to tell you this, but…I need to talk to someone. Mom, I had an abortion."

As the words rolled off my tongue, I could see the confusion in her face. She sat down across from me. "Honey, why didn't you tell me?"

"I didn't want you to stress about it or be mad. Chris said he doesn't want kids. So I did it for him. But now I resent him. Every little thing he does bothers me. And I'm depressed." I wiped tears from my face.

"Dila, listen to me. Never make a decision based on someone else's happiness. If he'd left you because you wouldn't get an abortion, trust me, we all would've helped you. You could have done it."

My mom was right. It was just all easier said than done.

"I have another confession." I put my head down. "I want to come back home and I think I'm still in love with Shaun."

Mom just laughed. "Phadila, it happens. You spent darn near your entire life with Shaun. It'll all come to pass, and when it does you'll be able to move on the way you should."

Mom was so right. I felt a little better as we started back cleaning the kitchen. Afterward we joined the rest of the family in the living room to watch movies and enjoy some quality time together. It was a great day.

A few days later, my prayer to be able to spend more time with my family was granted. I only needed two classes to graduate, meaning I didn't have to do a full last year. I decided to take the first semester off and finish in the spring. I also decided to accept a job offer in New York, at one of the biggest business law firms in the US. It paid well, and I needed all the experience I could get.

Before I left for New York, I needed to talk it over with Chris. Regardless of how he felt, I was going to leave. I waited for him to come home from work one night, let him relax a bit, and then brought up the topic.

"Chris, I want to talk to you." I said.

"What's up?" He added as if he was interested in what I had to say.

"You know I have a semester off from school, right?"

I continued. "Well, I miss my family, and my dad got me a job for the semester, so I'm going to go back to New York, just until this semester is over." I waited for his reply.

"If that's what you want. I mean, clearly you've already planned it. What do you want me to say?"

"I want you to be okay with my decision."

He picked up the remote and began flipping TV channels. "Do what you need to do."

So I did. And for the first time I didn't feel sorry about it.

* * *

Two weeks later I landed in New York and started working. I wanted to soak up all the knowledge I could. My job allowed me to meet some of the most important people in the business and established great relationships. I worked hard as a junior lawyer and when it was almost time for the spring semester to start, I didn't want to leave. The experience had given me so much more knowledge than I'd gained at school and my internship combined. It made me much more confident about someday starting my own firm. Apparently I made a great impression on the company and its clients as well.

"Phadila, do you mind if I talk to you?" my manager, Bill, said over the phone.

"Yes, I'll be right there!" I hung up the phone, walked into his office, and took a seat.

"I must say it has been a complete pleasure working with you."

I got nervous, assuming there was going to be a problem. "Thank you. I've enjoyed being here."

"I understand that you have to leave at the end of the month to return to school."

"Yes, I do. I'll graduate this semester."

"I know. Congrats!" Bill said. "I want to know if there's a possibility that you would fly home on weekends and work here. I also would love to offer you a full-time position once you graduate."

In complete shock I replied, "Of course!"

"Great! The company will pay for your flying back and forth. I'll have it written up in a contract for you before you head back to Cambridge."

"Thank you so much," I said. I was still a bit nervous as I walked back to my office. This position was perfect, and I was getting all the experience I needed, so of course I accepted the offer.

I worked hard at my job and spent every available minute with my family. Once the end of the month came I flew back to Cambridge. I had a taxi pick me up from the airport since Chris was at work. I got home and took a shower and got comfy in bed.

Chapter 19

During my last semester of school I worked in New York on the weekends, and spent a lot of time researching business law firms. Graduation was right around the corner and everything was smooth sailing.

I spoke to my family almost daily. Everyone was excited about me coming back home to New York, except Chris. As much as I cared about him, at this point I could care less how he felt. I had to do what was best for me.

"Phadila, you're not really good at communicating," he said one morning as I got dressed to go pick up my sister from the airport.

"What? Why would you say that?"

"You never include me in any of your plans."

"Chris, what are you talking about?"

"You didn't think it was important to tell me your sister was coming to visit for a week?"

I put on my jacket. "Well, I could have told you that my sister was coming, you're right, and I apologize, but either way she's coming and I don't feel that I need to make an announcement because she is my sister."

He looked angry. "Well maybe you need to start paying bills too."

"What does that have to do with anything?" I grabbed my cell phone off the dresser and walked out.

The airport was not far from my house and when I arrived, to my surprise, Phalana had her son Tony with her and Justin.

"Oh my God!" I shouted as I pulled up to the loading deck. I couldn't believe my eyes. It was Justin! I hadn't seen him since the day Shaun and I had broken up. He looked like a healthy and happy seven years old.

I put the car in park and jumped out. "Justin! Oh my goodness, how are you?" I pulled him to me and then held him away to get another look at him.

"Dila!" he said, putting his arms around my neck tightly. "I missed you."

"I missed you too." I was almost in tears.

"Hi, Auntie Dila!" my nephew Tony said.

"Tony, love, how are you?" I said.

"I'm good."

"Ma'am, I need you to move your car," a female cop said as I embraced my sister.

"Yes!" I replied happily. We all grabbed the luggage and threw it in the back of my Mercedes truck. I jetted back onto the freeway toward home.

I smiled at my sister. "Thanks for the surprise."

"No problem." She smiled back. "I watch Justin all the time when Shaun is out of town."

"Really? You never told me that." I thought for a moment. "Shaun's out of town now? For how long?"

"He's in Europe. He'll be there for about three months I think. Girl, I don't remember." She didn't seem very concerned.

Once home I made some breakfast. As I cooked Justin walked into the kitchen and sat at the table.

"Hi," he said, rubbing his eyes.

"Hi," I replied, opening the fridge. "Would you like something to drink?"

"No, no. I can wait for everyone else." He replied.

"Dila," he said. "I always wanted to know, why did we have to leave?"

An electric shock went through my body. I didn't want to say the wrong thing. He was still a child. He didn't need to know.

"Well, Justin, sometimes things between adults don't work out the way you plan them, or how you hope they'll be. I never wanted to let you go. You meant a lot to me. At the same time, I felt like I didn't have any right to keep you. Sometimes things aren't meant to be even when we want them to be."

"Yeah, I understand."

I turned my back and looked out the window as I stirred eggs in a bowl.

"Sometimes I wish I could have stayed with you," he went on. "My dad travels a lot, and I hate his new girlfriend."

My heart jumped into my throat. I turned around. "Well, you can't like everyone." I tried to smile, but it didn't work so I went over to the stove.

Chris walked into the kitchen, patted my butt, and took a seat at the counter.

"Hi, Justin. How are you?" he asked.

"Good," Justin replied. He didn't seem to take too well to Chris.

After breakfast all of us except Chris walked to the community center down the block so the kids could run around and Phalana and I could work out. As I ran on the treadmill, I couldn't take my mind off of my conversation with Justin. I realized I had never dealt with the breakup with Shaun. I found it easier to consume myself in my work and school to cope. The possibility of seeing Shaun gives me butterflies. But it was inevitable.

"I'm glad you were excited to see Justin," Phalana said as she speed-walked on the next treadmill over. "I thought bringing him might make things uncomfortable, especially for Chris."

"I think Chris is a little upset that I still have some connection to Shaun, but he'll have to get over it," I said. "I'm just happy to see Justin. I never expected to see him again."

"I feel you. Is Chris okay with that?"

"I don't know. I haven't talked to him about it, and I probably won't."

"Is he going to New York with you?"

"I don't know."

"Do you want him to?

I thought about it while I set the treadmill to a faster pace. "Yes, but if he doesn't want to, I won't be hurt."

"Hey, it is what it is. Shaun has a new girlfriend, though. And she's a total witch."

"Justin mentioned her."

"Phadila, do you miss Shaun?"

I thought again. How much time had I spent pondering that question? "I miss who he was to me before all of his success. He had a lot of characteristics I wanted in my future husband. I was willing to accept his faults because I wanted him in my life."

"His potential I'm sure helped a lot?" Phalana stated.

"Maybe so. I'm not really sure. I never really sat down and thought about it. I just consumed myself in work and school so much I didn't have to."

"Well, you may be surprised. He's changed a bit. I think this girlfriend has shown him he had something good with you. He always asks about you too. It gets annoying sometimes."

She smirked at me, and I smiled back. It did make me feel good to know Shaun still cared about me.

We continued working out for an hour, then went into the playroom with the kids and relaxed.

Throughout the week I took Phalana, my nephew, and Justin to museums and different tourist spots. They seemed to have had a good time in Cambridge.

The week flew by so fast, before I knew it I was taking them back to the airport. I talked to Justin on the phone almost every day. He was a good kid and had nothing to do with the issues between his father and me. I actually felt bad for walking out of his life. I tried to make it up to him by seeing him when I was in New York on the weekends, and when spring break came around I spent that with him too. "So what do you have planned for this week besides work?" Chris asked as I showered the morning I was going to leave.

"I don't know. I'm going to spend a lot of time with my family for sure. You should come. We could get our families together for dinner or something."

"Right your family, my family, and Shaun's family."

I peeked through the shower curtain. "You're such an ass. I didn't find that funny."

"But your families are so close."

"We are, but do you have to make it a bigger issue than it really is? Get over it. His sisters are married to my brothers and our moms are best friends." I turned off the water and got out of the shower.

"Exactly! So I should be asking what do you and Shaun have planned?"

Now that irritated me. "Nothing! I haven't seen Shaun in so long I don't even know what I would say if I did see him." I walked into the bedroom to get dressed. "Chris, I don't understand why you make so much out of my having dated Shaun and the possibility of us being cool one day. You make a bigger deal about it than I do."

"Well, let me see. You dated dang near your whole life, your families are extremely close, and you told me you're still in love with him."

I rolled my eyes as I pulled my hair back into a ponytail. "That was so long ago. So get over it!"

I grabbed my luggage just as Sheena and her son Jason Jr. Knocked on the front door. Chris helped us carry our luggage to the car. He also drove us to the airport in silence and dropping us off with no goodbye. When we landed in New York, my first order of business was to go to a meeting for my job. I dropped Sheena and Jason Jr. off at my parent's house and headed to the office.

"Phadila. How are you doing?" Bill, my manager, asked.

"I'm good, Bill. How are you doing?" I wasn't really in a talking mood. I sat in the meeting, which was two hours long and absolutely boring. No one in the room paid attention. I spent the whole time doodling on a piece of paper and wondering what I would call my company if I got the chance to start one. I decided to stick with my last name LombardiJones & Co. It worked better than anything.

Once the meeting was over I met with the owner of a building I was trying to purchase.

When I arrived a realtor and an inspector were there as well. During the meeting we talked about possible renovations.

"I love the high ceilings and the archway of the door. I don't want to do anything that would take away from the historic look of the building," I said to the inspector.

"Yeah, I was just thinking about how beautiful they are." He said. "They add a lot of personality. You know, the room is actually huge. You could maybe make one half of it a storage room or a place where you keep files because there's not much storage space."

"That would be a good idea. When I used this building, this was the conference room because it was so big," the owner stated.

"Also we need more windows. I hate my office at work now, I have zero windows. It reminds me of confinement," I said. The owner and agent laughed. They had no clue about my past of course.

"If everything is good, how would you like to work out the payments?"

"Cash," I said with a smile. "In full. No payments." Both he and the owner looked stunned. "In fact, I can go get it now and meet you at your office."

I got the money from my safe at Grams's house, met with the realtor and owner, then took my family out to dinner to celebrate.

"I'm extremely proud of you," my mom said. "You've taken risks to put yourself in a position that allows you to be your own person."

"Your mom is right," Dad said. "You have more passion and drive than we ever imagined. All we ever wanted was a job and a happy family. You want more, and that's what God has given you. We're both very proud," He raised his glass to toast the moment. We all followed suit.

My brother and I looked at each other and smiled. My parent's never missed a moment to tell us how proud they were of us.

In the middle of the conversation, my phone rang. "Hello?" I answered.

"Hi, babe." It was Chris. "So what's going on? You haven't called me to let me know that you made it."

"My bad. I've been so busy. I'm here! I'm eating lunch with my brother, my parents, and Sheena right now." I hoped he would insist that I called him back later.

"Okay. Tell them I say hello."

"I will," I replied.

"So what else do you have planned for this week?"

"Work and shooting the breeze," I told him. "That's all I have planned. Now, I'm going to have to call you back." It felt rude to talk on the phone while everyone was eating. "I love you," I added, then hung up the phone.

I didn't call him back that night, and I didn't call him much for the rest of the week. I was over his antics, and I was sure he was over mine as well.

I spent the rest of my time in New York with my family and Justin, and working on my business plan. I was actually so excited about buying the building I spent the last two nights sleeping on the floor of my new building. On my last day in New York, Sheena and I met up with my brother to go over the blueprints he had come up with. Then Sheena and I went to the public library to do some research and type up a mock business plan. We stayed in the library for about five hours. Until it was time to pick Jason Jr. up from my parent's house and head for the airport. I finally decided to call Chris while I walked to our gate.

"We'll be home in a while," I said, trying to figure out his mood.

"That's good. I'll pick you up." He had zero emotion in his voice.

"Is everything okay?"

"You tell me." He wasn't happy, and I knew I hear about when I got home.

"Well, I'll see you soon."

He hung up before I could say "I love you."

★★★

Chris was there when we landed in Cambridge, and he was in the same mood. He didn't say a word, not even when I asked him again if things were okay. I was concerned, but at the same time I wasn't. I needed to focus on my finals for school, which was rapidly coming to an end.

As soon as we got home I went to my bedroom to study. Mom called while I was reading.

"We're on three-way with all your sisters," she said, which meant something was up. "We were just talking about how excited we are for your graduation."

"I'm excited too to see all of you guys again."

"Well, as you may already know," Phalana said, "Justin's coming too with Teza and Haji."

"I know. I'm glad he'll be there. But why are you telling me? Is there something more to it?"

"Okay, I'm just going to say it," said my friend Randy. "Shaun wants to come. He wants to sit down and talk to you about being back in Justin's life as his mother figure."

I drew a blank. Chris passed me going on his way to the kitchen, so I waited to reply.

"Um, I don't know about all that," I said, keeping my voice low. "I will have to get back to you."

Everyone was quiet.

"There's also no need to make reservations, because we're all going to cook dinner," my mom said.

"That's nice, Mom, I really can't wait to come back to New York," I said, not really knowing where the conversation was going. They all talked about my graduation day plans and I hardly said a word. My mind raced all over the place about the possibility of Shuan coming and how Chris would handle it.

What could come out of this? More importantly, how would Chris react?

Chapter 20

The night before my graduation, I hardly slept. I tossed and turned for hours. I felt guilty that I hadn't talked to Chris yet about Shaun's coming in for the ceremony, but then again, I didn't think it was such a big deal not to tell him. Deep down I am overjoyed to see him, though I'm sure I'll play it cool. No matter what, I have to promise myself that I would not fall apart when I see him, especially with all my family and friends in town. Hopefully no one would mention Shaun to Chris until I found the words to tell him myself.

Graduation started at 9 a.m., but I had to be at the venue by 7 a.m. I woke up around 6 a.m., made breakfast, got ready, and left a little after six thirty. I sent a mass text message to everyone's phone with the directions.

When I arrived at the venue, everyone in my class was standing around waiting for their seating arrangements. I spoke to a few classmate until my cell phone rang. The number was unknown, but I answered anyway.

"Hi, Phadila," Shaun said, his voice extremely soft.

"Oh, hi. What's going on?" I asked, trying not to sound too excited.

"Nothing much. I just wanted to call and congratulate you. And say thank you for allowing me to be a part of your big day."

"Thank you. And you're welcome. I'm glad you wanted to be involved."

The conversation didn't last long; I didn't have much time, which was a relief for my nerves. But the call added to my already discombobulated thought process as I repeatedly read my valedictory speech to myself.

"Ugh, I need a drink," I said.

"Here." The girl next to me handed me a pint-size bottle of gin. I took a sip, and popped some gun in my mouth to cover the scent.

When the ceremony started I was so bored out of my mind that I daydreamed all the way up until my speech. As I stood to walk to the podium, my body quivered. Nervously I read my speech.

"I would like to thank my family and all of my peers who are like family for supporting each other's dreams. "

My speech wasn't the best, but I was proud of what I had done. I looked around and absorbed the moment. Seeing what I had accomplished made me extremely proud of myself. After my speech the ceremony continued on just as boring as it was. I had no clue what was going on or what was being said; by the time I caught up everyone was throwing their caps in the air and the school president was announcing us as graduates. I decided to keep my cap on and go looking for my family. I passed a few classmates and gave several congrats, but before I could turn my head, my brother grabbed me so tight in a hug that I almost lost focus.

"Congrats, little sis," Ohaji said, kissing my cheek.

"Thanks, brother," I said.

"Congrats, babe!" Chris said, hugging me tighter than ever.

"Thanks."

My brother, Chris, and I talked and little by little the rest of the family all approached. I hugged and kissed everyone, and thanked them each for their kind words, but in the midst of my glory I spotted Shaun out the corner of my eye. I acted as if I didn't notice him approaching. Chris did, though. He grabbed my waist a little closer as a reaction to seeing Shaun approach us.. Suddenly I felt a small tug of war between the two men as Shaun's hand pulling me away from Chris for a hug.

"Congrats," he whispered in my ear.

"Thank you!" I said, backing away and reaching to pick up Justin.

"Shaun, nice to see you," Chris said, reaching out to shake his hand. "I didn't know you were coming."

"What's up, Chris? You're just as surprised as I am. I didn't expect to see you here with Phadila."

"Well, let's go get something to eat," Sheena said, quickly assessing the situation and its awkward possibilities. We all agreed and headed for out cars to leave.

"That seemed to go well," I said to Phalana as we buckled in our seatbelts in my car.

She laughed. "Phadila, I can't believe you didn't tell Chris Shaun was coming. It's going to get ugly."

"I don't think so." I replied knowing this could go either way.

Unsure of what could happen it took me no time to get home. I wanted to talk to Chris before things went any further. But when I walked in there were people everywhere, and the scent of my Mom's cooking filled the whole house. I immediately got distracted as I rushed to my room to change my clothes and get ready for a good ol' time.

"So you didn't feel it was necessary to tell me Shaun was coming?" Chris asked as he closed the bedroom door behind him.

"It's not that serious, Chris. My mom told me he *wanted* to come. She never said he *was* coming. So technically I didn't know."

"Technically you knew there was a possibility!" He came closer to me grabbing my waistline.

"What are you so worried about? We're not getting back together. He's just here as family. As I always make a point to tell you, get over it." I turned to kiss him on the lips.

"I won't!" We both walked out of the room making our way to the back patio. There were even more people in the backyard. Chris followed, but I kept my back turned to him.

"You need to get over yourself and be real with me," he said. I didn't acknowledge him.

"Everyone please gather around the table in the backyard to bless the food!" My mom yelled from inside the house. Everyone quickly poured out and formed a circle.

"Before I bless the food," my dad said, "I want everyone to go around and say something short about Phadila."

"Phadila, I'm so proud of you, and I love you!"
One by one the people in the circle spoke, each of them bringing me to tears. Finally dad blessed the food and everyone began to make their plates. I fixed two for myself. We all talked, laughed, and enjoyed each other's company whether we knew one another or not.

As the night wore on, people came and went. We ate, drank, and played games. At one point Shaun came by and signaled for me to step into the guest bedroom. I smiled and went.

"What's up?" I asked.

"I've wanted to talk to you for a while now about the way things went down in the past, and about my appreciation for everything you've done for me and Justin. I know this may not be a good day to do it, but I don't think there will ever really be a good enough day."

I nodded in agreeing as he continued. "First I want to apologize for taking advantage of the relationship, your trust, and your kindness. Second I want to apologize for not being man enough to come to you and say I wasn't happy. It took space for me to come to realize you were everything I needed."

I shrugged my shoulders and took a sip of my drink. Shaun went on. "I also want to thank you for being there for my son and loving him as your own, even when we both were a bit unlovable."

I slowly started daydreaming. I tend to have that problem when people don't just get to the point. As he continued to speak, I got a little turned on. Maybe it was the drinks. I don't know but I could not listen to his drawn out apology any longer so I raised my finger as if we were in church to interrupt.

"Shaun, thank you. I really appreciate your apology. I'm not mad at you. I am just disappointed. I put so much of myself into you and I was let down. I was selfish to not understand that people's needs and wants change. And I was wrong trying to force you to love me the way I wanted you to without expressing to you what I needed. I wanted us to have everything my parents had and more. I guess the idea of love was more appealing for me, and that was my fault. You're a good person. For things to happen the way they did at the time was hurtful and devastating. I felt like you completely got caught up in your lifestyle and I found myself lost in trying to be someone you could find easy to love. I learned a lot about myself and I've moved on. For the most part, I'm good."

I felt like a huge weight had been lifted off my shoulders.

"Dila," Shaun went on, "you don't know what I have been through these past couple of years.

It all has helped me realize how amazing you are. So again, thank you, and I'm sorry."

I stood up, trying to bring the conversation to a close. There wasn't much else I needed to say. And I just wasn't feeling it but Shaun continued talking.

"I want to know, will you be my friend again? And when you move back home, will you help me with Justin? He adores you so much; I would love to maybe get things back to how they were before." He grabbed my hand.

Laughing, "what are we six? Is there a box for me to check as well? Of course I will," I replied continuing. "We can be friends again. Like I said you're a good person. We all act selfishly sometimes. We're human. A lot of our problems were my fault as well. I turned a blind eye to a lot of things I should have just communicated to you but you live and learn."

He reached out to hug me. "It's all good. But I do plan on wearing you down and getting rid of Chris. How did you even hook up with him?"

I didn't answer. I just got up and walked back to the kitchen for another drink. Chris was in the hallway, he didn't look very happy. I tried to kiss him but he pulled away.

"What?" I asked.

"You're killing me," he replied.

"There's nothing to worry about. It's not like that at all."

"Do you think I believe that? Phadila, you spent most of your life in love with Shaun. You broke up and he was nowhere to be found. All of a sudden Justin comes to visit with your sister and now you're going home on weekends and Justin is staying with you. Shaun could be there too for all I know. And now he's at your graduation party."

I took a deep breath. Chris was so good at making so much out of something so little. "This is the first time I've seen Shaun. My family invited him. I don't want to be with him." I stepped forward to kiss him again, hoping it would make things okay.

"Clearly I'm not important enough for you to think you should tell me anything that's going on in your life."

"Chris, you are important. But today is my day, and I'm not going to entertain this conversation right now please." I turned to walk away.

"Funny. You just entertained a conversation with your ex."

As I turned to react, Chris grabbed his keys off the counter and walked out the front door. I watched him out the front window driving off. I tried to call him several times. Not once did he answer. That night was the last time I saw or spoke to Chris. Honestly as much as it tore me apart, I was tired. It was time to get back to myself.

Chapter 21

After graduation things were all over the place. I worked full-time at the law firm and I kept Justin on weekends and when Shaun was out of town.

The renovations of the building I bought were underway. Months and days dragged on into two years. I had gotten so caught up in working that I had forgotten about my dream. One morning I woke up in a sweat and sat on the edge of my bed. It was time to make some serious changes. I was getting to old.

As I got ready for work, I had the biggest headache known to man. I took two Tylenols and hopped into the shower. I jetted through the morning traffic and got to work five minutes early.

In the elevator, I noticed the mail boy smiling at me a little more than usual.

"Congratulations!" He said. I had no idea what he was talking about, but he was the only cute black man in the entire company, so I smiled back replying, "Thank you."

Just as I was about to walk into my office, Sheena came in to catch me up on all the company gossip as she did every Monday morning.

"Dang, Dila. The party last night was great. You were so drunk!" I had forgotten about my co-workers birthday party the night before.

"Yeah, and I have the headache to prove it. What are you so freaking chipper about? All the bouncing is making me sick to my stomach."

"Oh you haven't heard?"

"Heard what?" I replied while looking through my appointments for the day.

"You're one of three people up for partner at the firm!"

"Huh?" I replied semi excited on the inside. "I guess that explains why the mail boy congratulated me in the elevator."

"You talked to the mail boy? Dang, I can't even get him to notice me. But anyway, you're up against Corey Emerson, the cokehead, and Johnny

Boyd, the pervert. Don't worry. You're the best candidate. You got this. No worries. And if they don't pick you, girl, we'll say they're racist."Sheena laughed seriously.

I had a desk full of phone appointments that before I knew it, I had worked through my lunch break. Once I noticed it my stomach started growling as I began to search my desk for change to get something out of the vending machine. I walked into the break room to notice the CEO Mr. Fowler. "How are you doing today sir?" I said reaching for my candy out of the machine. "Hi Phadila, I'm doing fine." He replied. "That's good." I responded. He continued to speak. "Congrats. However we've already made our decision and we've actually going to go with Corey." I leaned against the soda machine replying,"But sir I'm one of your best workers, especially better than Corey." I replied. "Yes I know but this company has a standard and promoting him would actually make us look good." Mr. Fowler was serious. I stood there in shock.

"Look good as far as what?" I asked. "He is a male and he knows how to fit into the board of directors. You know business." Mr. Fowler replied walking out of the break room.

Suddenly I was no longer hungry. In fact I was furious. I stormed back to my office and to hear my cell phone ringing.

"Phadila, the CEO would like you to join him in the conference room." It was his personal assistant calling about the meeting.

"Thank you, I will be there." I tried to pull myself together. I wished I hadn't went the break room. I wish I wasn't only one of five women in the entire firm. I wished I was white and male.

I walked into the conference room and took a seat. Corey was there, Johnny was there and the company's partners.

"Phadila," the CEO said. "Glad you could join us. You're a little late, but that's okay." The joke burned my soul even more. "I've invited you all to this meeting because you're all up for a big promotion to partner. We've made a decision and we want to share it with you all."

He rambled on about how they came to their decision, but I couldn't stop playing back the break room conversation in my head. I kept thinking; *I hate this job. I hate this job!* "Congratulations!" I turned to Corey with my hand out for a hand shake.

"Phadila, we haven't announced who we've picked." The CEO glared at me.

"It's okay. I was already told in the break room by Mr. Fowler that Johnny and I never had a chance because we don't fit into the company's image."

It felt so good to stand up to him, though I was worried as hell about my job. As I excused myself from the meeting, butterflies flew like crazy in my stomach.

When I got back to my office, Sheena was there. "Um, hello! You're supposed to be in a meeting accepting your position. What are you doing?" she asked.

"I'm not old enough, white enough, or male enough. I'm just filling a space. Makes me feel like crap!" Tears rushed down my face, warming my cheeks.

"Phadila!" my manager, Bill, rushed into my office. Sheena tiptoed out. "What you did in there shouldn't have been done. You embarrassed the company for God shake."

As he yelled, I gathered my things to leave.

"What are you doing?" he asked.

"If you want to fire me I understand but what I don't understand is how is it I've gotten comfortable working for a company that can't see me as a partner because I was born a woman?"

I stood behind my desk, my cell phone in my hand. "I'm one of the top three lawyers in this firm. I have more successes than anyone here including you, but I don't have a fair chance at being any more than what I am. I come in day in and day out, working hard and trying to make everyone who's not black comfortable with who I am. Why do I bother? Why am I still here?"

Even I was shocked by my response. I wanted to pat myself on the back. I knew Bill was surprised too.

And he made it apparent that my actions were not okay. "Phadila, there's a time and place for everything. You know that better than anyone." He continued, "You know what? Take the rest of the day off. We'll talk about it in the morning." He left and closed my office door behind him.

I grabbed my things and headed to my car to just sit there. I had no clue what I would do if I lost this job. I started the ignition and drove out into traffic. I headed home still unsettled, even worried. *Should I file a lawsuit against the company?* I thought. *But for what?* To make them hire more blacks and women so they wouldn't appear not to discriminative.

I got home stretched out across my living room couch and stared at the white walls. I needed to talk to someone about this. I called my dad.

"Hey, love," he said when he picked up.

"Dad, I need to talk to you about something."

"Hold on a minute, Phadila. Your mom wants to talk to you."

"Okay," I replied.

"Hi, honey, how are you?" Mom asked. "Have you talked to your brothers or your sister yet?"

"No, why?"

"Well, I need to tell you something important." The most exciting part of my mom's day was the Oprah Winfrey show. I knew what she had to tell me couldn't be that deep. "Honey, Grams passed away."

My chest felt like it collapsed.

"We're not sure why yet, but if it makes it any better, she passed away in her sleep."

The more she said, the tighter my chest felt and the weaker I grew.

"Phadila, are you still there?"

"Yes, Mom. Um, let me call you back, please." I hung up without waiting for her reply. I didn't want to believe it. I called Grams's house phone several times, hoping she would pick up. I got the voicemail each time falling deeper and deeper into sadness.

I spent the entire night balled up in a knot full of tears. I didn't answer my phone and I didn't want to be around anyone.

The next morning I went into work a little easier on the attitude, Bill was waiting for me as I stepped off the elevator.

"Phadila, can I talk to you?"

"Sure." I threw my hands up. I wasn't in the mood to deal with this really.

He took me into his office. "Is everything okay?" he asked.

"Everything is good. Just got some really bad news and I'm trying to figure out how to deal with it. Why? What's up?"

"Well, I understand you were upset yesterday, and I want to apologize. I'm not going to fire you because you one of the best lawyer's we have. You had every right to act the way you did. Just not in that setting. The CEO wants me to let you go, but I'm keeping you."

"Thank you. I appreciate your support. I do need a favor, however." I attempted to act as if I cared whether or not I still had a job or not.

"Yes, what is it?" Bill sat forward in his seat.

"My grandma passed away and I need some time off." I caught my tears as they began to run rapidly down my face.

"Oh my, I'm sorry to hear that. Yes, of course. Take however long you need."

Why did he say that? I thought. I immediately excused myself to my car and made it home where could isolated myself for days. At least until my mom pulled me out to help the rest of the family clean out Gram's house. Every box held a story or memories that led to laughs and eventually tears. My dad rented a U-Haul to take away the furniture that no one could really use.

Because I was so out of it I just piled it all in the truck.

"You need help with that?" a baritone voice asked as I struggled to hoist a chair up. I looked up and to my surprise there was Chris. I hadn't seen him since he walked out on me.

"How are you?" I threw the chair onto the truck and turned to give him my undivided attention."I'm good," I replied. "You look good." He responded.

Every ounce of me wanted to fall into his arms and slap the taste out of his face. "Thank you. You don't look bad yourself."

"Listen, I'm sorry about your Grams. I know how much she meant to you. I'm visiting my mom, I saw ya'll over here and thought I would offer to help you clean out the house. Thought you might need an extra hand?"

"That's nice," I replied with a smirk. For an instant forgetting about what was going on around me. "My hand *is* getting a little tired."

"Well, I'm that guy."

"Hi," I heard a little girl's voice say from the side of the truck. I looked around to see who was speaking.

"Dila, this is my daughter, Jessica," Chris said.

I stood there stiff as a statue. "Wow, you have a kid?"

"Yes. She's the love of my life."

I became so upset in that moment in that I couldn't move my body to react.

"Phadila! Move out the way," my brother Christian called as he came through carrying another chair. I took that opportunity to get back to cleaning to avoid having to talk any more to Chris.

"What's up, Chris? How are you doing?" Christian asked as I began to walk away. I caught Chris's eye unwittingly but we didn't say much after he introduced his daughter. I couldn't believe he had a child after telling me he never wanted to have any. I kept my distance as he helped us pack the truck. I didn't want to find out anything else.

The funeral was the next day I could barely pull myself out of bed. My body was tired and in so much pain from lifting boxes at Grams's. But I had finally gotten my first full night of sleep in days. When I was finally able to sit up at the edge of my bed, I reminisced about the good times I had with Grams. I picked up the phone.

"Hi, Mom," I said. "I'm about to get ready now and head that way. Is there anything we need?"

"No, honey, everything is okay. Just get over here because almost everyone is on their way." Mom always knew how to tell me to speed it up without actually saying it.

"I'll be there in a few." I reached over to the nightstand to lay down my phone. I washed, got dressed, and hurried over to my parent's house. I pulled into the driveway to find I was indeed the last to get there, with just enough time for the family limo to drive off. I got into a limo with my parents; as I heard Chris's voice yet again.

"Phadila, God's going to take care of it for you."

"Shut up," I said under my breath. We rode to the funeral service in complete silence, which was unusual for my family. We pulled up to the church and we made our way in.

"You okay?" Phalana asked, grabbing my hand as we marched to our seats.

"As good as I will be, you?"

"No, but I'm going to be. She's in a better place."

A few minutes later the service began.

"Please be seated," the pastor announced from the pulpit. "We're going to start the service." People rushed to their seats as some stood alongside the church walls.

My cousin Sheila got up to lead the service. "Good afternoon and welcome to the home going celebration of Mrs. Sallie Joann Richardson, known to many as Grams. If you knew her, you know she didn't want this to be a sad occasion but a joyous one." Sheila's voice trembled. "Now, that may be a little hard, but Grams always said a hard head makes a soft behind, and I'm far too old for a spanking."

Sheila was the perfect MC, she kept everyone laughing. It was a long funeral we sat through three solos and almost twenty more speeches about Grams. Finally there was the pastor's overly heavier than usual breathing during his sermon.

"The casket will be opened and each of you can pay your respects," he said at last. One by one we went up and looked at Grams in complete gratitude. Gram's death was the hardest thing for me to get over, yet at the same time it was every bit of the motivation I needed.

Chapter 22

September of the following year was a new beginning. I was finally a month away from my company's grand opening, and I turned in my two Weeks's notice at the law firm.

One Monday morning before I left, I rushed into my office late for a meeting. As Sheena helped me gather all of my paperwork, I listened to several voicemails.

"Hey, Phadila, it's Mr. Ball, the one working on your building. I need to talk to you as soon as possible. The building's renovations are complete!" I quickly pushed the stop button and looked at Sheena.

"Finished!" I repeated. She was just as happy as I was.

Once I got everything I needed, I rushed into the meeting only to realize it hadn't even started. Apparently everyone was running late, so I decided to step out in the hallway and call Mr. Ball back.

"Hey, so it's ready?" I said when he answered his phone.

"Yes, it is. If you like to you can come check it out." He replied. "I will be by as soon as I can." I replied walking back into the meeting.

When the meeting ended I went back to my office and typed up my resignation letter. I finished and didn't hesitate to take it to Bill's office.

"Hi, Bill, are you busy?" I asked, fixing my skirt.

"Phadila, I'm not busy at all. Come in. How are you?"

"Thanks, I'm good. Great, actually I want to talk to you about something." I said as I made myself comfortable in a chair.

"Shoot!" Bill replied with his trademark wink and gun.

"Well, Bill, I've come to inform you that this will be my last week with the company."

His face quickly went from smiling to frowning. "You're leaving the company?"

"I'll be starting a new position. I apologize for the last-minute notice."

"A new position, where?"

"My own company,"

He chuckled. "Your own company, Are you sure about that? I mean, you're the best worker we have, but where will you get the startup money? I'm not saying it can't happen…it's just…wow."

I smiled, though I wasn't really amused. "I already have the money. I'll be having an orientation for my new employees soon." I smiled. "I already have three possible major clients." I handed him my letter. He didn't seem pleased. "Oh yeah, and you must see my new office one day. It's in Manhattan. I own the building. I can see my old neighborhood from my office window. It's so cool."

I got up to walk out of the office as Bill continued,

"Yeah, that sounds great! Maybe I'll stop by to see it one day." Bill replied.

"Yes!" I shouted, walking back to my office.

* * *

I was leaving the office I hated walking into every morning with no resentment. It was the size of a laundry room with no windows. It was depressing and reminded me of being back in prison. Honestly I didn't need any reminders of that. Therefore I was beyond excited to be leaving.

I finished the week out anxiously packing up my office. I also noticed a change in Bill's attitude toward me. It was clear I wasn't a favorite anymore, if I ever really had been. When I spoke he acted as if he didn't hear me. On the other hand, some of my coworkers brought me gifts and handed me their resumes just in case I had anymore openings.

I didn't even bother showing up on Thursday which was my last day. I used the whole day to be lazy.

Friday evening I picked Justin up from Shaun's house because Shaun was headed out of town. Before I could see if Justin wanted a snack or anything he was in bed. I lit some candles and took a long, relaxing bubble bath, then sat in my home office and planned out the next couple of months.

I poured myself a glass of wine, my usual nightcap and kicked my feet up. I sat with my laptop in my lap, reading over a few e-mails Sheena had set up for me for meetings with possible clients. I began researching the companies on the net and taking notes. Once I got enough information about each company, I called it a night.

The next morning I went straight to my office building for my first potential client, "Good morning," I said to the members of the Olympic organization. "Welcome to LombardiJones.

Let me tell you about our company." They seemed impressed, and by 10:00 a.m., I had signed my first client for nearly $10 million a year. I was on cloud nine. The pressure was on, but I was ready.

"Dila are you ready? " Sheena asked as she popped her head in my office door.

"More than ever," I replied, fixing my suit as I headed back to the conference room, where I introduced myself to the next potential client. I got right down to business. I went through the same process as I had in the first meeting. *If it isn't broke, don't fix it,* I thought. I even added a little more information than I had in the first one.

The meeting ended fifteen minutes earlier than expected and surprisingly the clients didn't have a lot of questions. They were very impressed; before I could ask if there was anything specific they were looking for, each person had already signed the contract. I was amazed; this was just too easy I thought. Sheena and I again went over everything just so they would know our commitment as well as what we expected from them. We engaged in small talked with the clients for a few minutes and then I walked them out.

I went back into my office elated.

"Wow, Dila!" Sheena came running into my office, closing the door behind her.

"I know, I know. Can you believe what's happened today? Thank you so much." I grabbed her for a hug and we both jumped up and down screaming.

"Girl, you know you don't need to thank me. I just brought them in. You sealed the deal."

I looked down at my watch. "I have to go pick up Justin, but come over later. We can have a drink or two to celebrate."

"Yes, you know I will. I have to go pick up Jason Jr., but I will be there."

* * *

When I pulled up to Justin's school, he sat on the stoop with some friends.

"How was your day?" I asked as he got into the car.

"It was fun. We got to cut open a frog." He was way too excited about killing a frog.

"That sounds like fun," I replied jokingly. The whole ride home he explained the process in detail. When we got home, I got comfortable, helped Justin with his homework, and ordered his favorite pepperoni pizza. Just as the delivery man was leaving, Sheena called.

"Dila, we're going to have to reschedule. Jason Jr. has a high fever and I'm taking him to the emergency room," she said all before I could say hello.

"Oh, no, I hope he's okay. Do you need me to come too?"

"No, girl. Enjoy your day. I'll take care of this."

Justin and I ate our pizza and watched cartoons until he fell asleep. After putting him to bed, I took a shower and relaxed on the couch, watching basketball with a glass of wine. Three minutes before halftime, there was a knock at the door.

"Who is it?" I asked.

"Shaun!" the voice on the other side replied.

I opened the door. "Hey, what's up? I thought you were out of town?"

"I got back early," he said as he stepped inside. "I know it's a little late, but can I talk to you?"

"You're already in, so why not? You want some pizza? Or wine?"

"Nah, I'm good. Thanks."

I sat back down on the couch as he sat in front of me on the coffee table. "Dila, I've been thinking for the past few months about a lot of things."

I poured more wine into my glass. My mind went in and out of the conversation; I really didn't want to have it again. But clearly he hasn't gotten his point across. A bit aroused thanks to my wine, when he grabbed my hand it brought my focus back to the conversation. Not really to the conversation because I was having a different one in my mind.

"Dila, I will do anything, therapy, whatever," he said, moving his hands to my thighs. I got a few butterflies in my stomach so I put my glass of wine down thinking just maybe I had enough to drink. I tried to imagine something else the more I watched his lips move up and down, I imagined kissing him even more.

"I just really want another chance to make things right. I miss you," he said.

Breathing a little harder, I fidgety got up to put the pizza box in the trash taking a swig of wine straight from the bottle nervously. I knew that this night was about to take a turn into the unknown.

"Dila, are you listening to me?" Shaun said as I walked back into the living room. He plopped his body in my red sofa. I attempted to step over his feet to get to the couch. Just as I was about to say something, he leaned over to kiss me. For a second I fought it, but the more I did, the more I melted in his arms. He softly kissed my lips, my cheek, and then my neck. His hands began to search my inner thighs pulling up my shirt to reveal my naked body. He cautiously grabbed my waist and pulled himself closer to me. Gradually sitting back in the chair pulling me So close I didn't resist. I kissed him back, caressing his face, his head, and his back as he slowly lifted me up as I placing my legs around his neck.

He started kissing my inner thigh, allowing his tongue and soft lips to touch every sensitive part of my glory. I took no time for me to reach my peak. Before I could come back to earth he was laying me down on the coffee table for more. He kissed my stomach and left no part of my body untouched.

We were in sync, he completely focused on pleasing me until the moment came to another peak. The more we kissed and caressed each other, the more I didn't want him to stop. I had forgotten all about Justin in the other room. Just as that thought ran through my mind. It was like the minute that thought ran through my mind it also ran through his. He became fidgety and worried. He slowly placed himself inside of me and began to stroke slowly, breathing harder and harder by the second. I was enjoying every bit of it. All of a sudden he rises up anxiously "I'm sorry. I shouldn't have done all that," he said, scratching his head.

"No, no… It was good… I mean, you're good… Well, you know what I mean." I couldn't focus on anything.

"Well, maybe I should go before Justin wakes up. Or do you want me to bring him home with me right now?"

I sat on the coffee table, looking up at him. "No, he can stay. I'll drop him off after school tomorrow." I pulled my shirt down ashamed. He grabbed his keys continuing to apologize as he walked toward the front door.

I softly followed him. Deep down inside I didn't want him to leave. In fact I wanted to jump back on him for another round. As he leaned in to kiss my neck, I whispered, "Stay."

"I can't," he said. "I want to, but I went about this all wrong. I just couldn't help myself."

"Don't help yourself, help me," I stood there somewhat vulnerable as he turned to walk out the door.

Chapter 23

I woke up the next morning with a different pep in my step, only to be brought back down to earth. *"Did we use a condom?"* I jumped out of bed rushing into the living room to search the couch, hoping to find at least a wrapper.

"Mom, is everything okay?" Justin asked, standing in the hallway, ready for school.

"Yes, everything is good, just looking for an earring." He continued to watch me,"I guess you're ready?" I asked taking a deep breath. I got dressed, rushed Justin to school, and headed to my office.

"Phadila, are you okay?" Sheena asked as I rushed by her desk, out of breath.

"Yes. Are the clients here? Are we ready?" I asked as I gathered everything I needed for the meeting.

"Yes, they just arrived." Sheena handed me a folder. I was so out of whack I zoomed through the first client meeting but making sure I answered every question they had. Once I finished, they didn't seem interested saying they'd get back to me in a few days. I was upset about not securing them but glad it had given me a moment to get last night off of my mind.

Once I got home later that night a thought occurred to me; maybe I should take the morning after pill better safe than sorry. I wrote it on my to-do list to go to the pharmacy and pick one up first things in the morning.

I felt a little more at ease after I poured myself a glass of juice and checked a few e-mails. I hadn't looked at them in about two weeks, so my inbox was full. Most were spam, but as I deleted them I came across one with the subject "Confidential Information." I opened and briefly skimmed through it. It was from the National Basketball Association.

Shocked I went back to the top to read it more carefully. To my surprise I was being contacted to be one of the marketing chairs members for the NBA. The e-mail stated I should call to set up a meeting with the board in LA.

Unsure of whether or not it was real, I called my dad as usual.

"Hey, Daddy," I said as he picked up the call.

"Hey, love. What's going on?"

"Well, I just opened my e-mail and I've been contacted to be one of the marketing companies for the NBA," I said slowly, making sure he didn't miss a word.

"What? That's amazing! You're going to accept the offer, right?"

"Well, the e-mail says to call as soon as possible. So I will call in the morning. Please don't tell anyone until we know for sure that it's real."

"Of course. I understand. I wonder who thought of you, out of all the people who could have been nominated. It's an honor."

"I know! I'm excited. I have butterflies." I took a deep breath to relax as I gave my dad all of the information. We then began to talk about the possibilities and how it would help with the success of LombardiJones.

After we finished talking, I continued going through the rest of my e-mails but none were as exciting. I printed out the e-mail from the NBA, folded it in half, and placed it in my Bible while saying a small prayer of hope.

After my moment of enthusiasm, I wrote out my to do list for the next day, then attempted to go to bed with a broken heart. Of course I spent the whole night crying because there was still no call, no anything for Shaun. I'm not sure why I was so emotional but I reminisced on all the years we spent building something that didn't work out. I tried to push the thoughts out my head and forced myself to sleep.

At five in the morning, my phone rang.

"Hello?" I answered. I was pissed. I had finally just gotten to sleep.

"Dila, you need to get up!" It was my sister-in-law, Teza. "Shaun and Justin are in the hospital. They got into a really bad car accident."

"It's okay, she's family," The bodyguard said while waving me into the parking lot.

"Thank you," I told him, although I was still a little ticked off at the rude policeman. I parked and stepped out my car swarmed by people from every angle. Cedric the bodyguard escorted me into the hospital and to the waiting room where both families sat. The spirit of the room was grim.

"What happened?" I asked Teza.

"They were hit by a drunk driver after Shaun picked Justin up from soccer tryouts."

"It's five-thirty in the morning, Teza. This didn't just happen. How come no one called me?"

"Phadila, calm down. We're all just finding out as well."

My mom wrapped her arms around me to calm me down. I felt a ball of fire boiling in my throat and tears began to roll down my face. I sat down and put my head in my palms to hide my face.

I remained with my head down until a doctor came out to give us a report on Justin and Shaun's recovery.

"I have some good news and some okay news," he announced. "Justin is doing great. He can go home." Doctor Williams said continuing, "On the other hand, Shaun will have to stay overnight just to make sure. You can see him, one at a time, but he may or may not be able to hear you."

Everyone sat in silence waiting their turn.

"So will he be okay?" Shaun's mother asked.

"He is fine, he is just a little banged up right now," the doctor said. "Thankfully he had on his seatbelt."

One by one we went in to see Shaun. I hadn't seen him since that night he came to my house, and in that moment I did everything in my power not to think create an awkward moment.

Why do hospitals always smell like death? I thought as I opened the door to his room. Justin sat at Shaun's side but jumped up and ran to me as I walked into the room. I reached down and gave him a huge hug, spinning him around in tears. That moment meant everything to me.

We walked hand in hand to Shaun's bedside as he slowly turned to look at me. "Hi," I said. "I just wanted to come and make sure everything is okay."

He smiled. "I'm good. I'm surprised you're here. I know you hate hospitals."

"Right but I need to be here. I'm glad that you're okay. Everyone's rooting for your recovery."

"Thanks, Dila. I appreciate it."

There was that awkward silence I wanted to avoid. He grabbed my hand. "You look good as always. Damn, I really messed up when I let you go, huh?"

I didn't want to take the conversation there. "Shaun, you're in the hospital. Don't worry about that now. Your recovery is more important." I smiled a little a bit flattered.

"But you look good too, even with your bumps and bruises."

"You're such an ass. Do you know that?" he replied "But that's what I love about you. You never hold any punches."

We held hands for a while until Justin and I said goodbye.

"How is he doing?" Shaun's mom asked, reaching out for Justin.

"He's good. Better than I expected. We had a nice conversation."

"Bet you did," Phalana said.

"What is that supposed to mean?"

"He's been talking about how much he's still in love with you. So I know you two had plenty to talk about."

I rolled my eyes and looked down at my watch. I had a photo shoot for marketing items for my new company. Phalana agreed to watch Justin while I was out. Cedric helped me get back to my car in one piece. After rushing across town, I arrived at the shoot five minutes late, but no one seemed to notice. I got dressed and got my makeup done while trying to stay focused. The photographer was in a bit of a rush, but I didn't mind. What was supposed to be a two-hour day soon came to an end in five hours. I was changing back into my own clothes when an email came through saying that the NBA wants to meet with me and others this coming Saturday, if that's okay. And that the tickets have been taken care of. I continued to put my clothes on and eventually leaving. I drove home with the meeting in Los Angeles on my mind. I got jitters when I realized that Monday was Lombardijones's grand opening.

I walked into the door. "There went the two days I had off before leaving for Los Angeles." I stated. Mrs. Gloria, my sister, my nephew Chris, Justin, and I all sat at the table to eating. Just before Justin's bedtime, I had him call Shaun.

"Hey, how are you doing? Better, I hope?" I asked.

"I'm good, thanks. Body's a little sore, but I'm alive."

"I'm calling so you can talk to Justin and to let you know I'm flying out to LA on Saturday for a big meeting. Justin is coming with me."

"That's cool. Good luck with that." We were silent for a moment.

"Well, here's Justin." I handed him the phone and grabbed another slice of pizza. They talked for thirty few minutes. Then Chris and Justin went to bed, Mrs. Gloria went home, and Phalana and I talked for hours. We ended up falling asleep in the living room, me on the couch and Phalana on the floor.

Chapter 24

"Oh my God!" I shouted, standing in line at the gate, waiting to get on my flight to California.

"Irresponsible!" I muttered to myself. I had forgotten to pick up the morning-after pill from the pharmacy. It was Saturday and it had been more than seventy-two hours, not to mention I was in the process of boarding my flight to California. There was nothing I could do.

I couldn't focus on anything else for the entire flight. I stared out the window, pissed off because I should have been more focused on my meeting. My dad handed me a folder full of the organization's history but I couldn't even stay focused on it eventually dozing off.

Once we landed we made our way through LAX. I wore a hoody and shades to keep a low profile. At the hotel Justin napped and I read up on my future client. Then I set the alarm and laid down for a nap.

An hour and a half later my dad was at my door, telling me to get ready for the meeting. All done up, I looked absolutely amazing. In the car I went over my notes again. At the company's building, we were greeted by Peter Cohen, the president of the organization.

"Hello, Phadila. Am I saying that right?" He shook my hand firmly.

"Hello. Yes. How are you?" I replied, turning to face my dad. "This is my father, George Lombardijones."

They shook hands and we proceeded to the nearby elevator.

"How was your trip?" Mr. Cohen asked, looking at both of us.

"It was great. Thank you," I responded, smiling. The elevator door opened and he led us in. We went up to a conference room full of older white men in suits. We greeted everyone at the table as we were seated. Peter passed around manila folders to everyone.

"Everyone is here therefore we will go ahead and get this meeting started," he said. I glanced around the room, wondering where I fit in. I repeatedly adjusted my seat and fumbled with my folder and pen unsure.

"Ms. Lombardijones," Mr. Cohen went on, "Ms. Lombardijones we feel that your company would be a great asset to our organization. You have a great deal of passion for the game and a wide understanding of the business. There are several other companies that will join with yours to help our organization from many different angles. We're extremely excited about what is to come and how combining various companies together will help our supporters take notice."

The Mr. Cohen took his seat. I looked around to see everyone's expressions. My dad was smiling from ear to ear.

One by one the men at the table spoke about why their company would be a great asset before I finally responded.

"I'm honored to be offered such an accolade," I said. "This truly means a lot to me because I love the game of basketball and I would love for my company to be a part of its success. My only concern is that I don't have a full understanding of what you're asking of me."

"Everything you need to know is in the folder in front of you," Mr. Cohen said. "Your contract is also in there. You can sit here for however long you need to and look over the contract but it must be signed by the end of today."

"That's not a problem at all."

Everyone stood, shook hands, and excused themselves, leaving me and my dad alone in the overly warm conference room. We carefully looked over the paperwork and talked it over before I made my final decision.

"Phadila," my dad said, sitting back in his chair, "you will be the only woman of color out of all the others. I'm saying this because I want you to understand how important this is. It's bigger than you."

"This is a dream Dad… I'm excited, honored, and I'm ready for whatever challenge this may bring my way."

Two hours later, after reviewing the contract again and making some changes, we walked into the president's office and handed it to him. He looked it over, then gave it to his assistant.

"April, can you make the changes to this contract and print it out please?"

She nodded politely and did as she was told. We engaged in small talk while we waited. Once she was done, my dad and I looked over the contract quickly to make sure everything was corrected, then we proceeded back to the conference room so everyone could sign.

"Thank you, Phadila!" Mr. Cohen said. It was official I was now one of the marketing companies for the NBA. We took pictures for the press and then my dad and I headed back to the hotel. I felt like I was walking on air until I passed a pregnant lady in the lobby replaying the night with Shaun in my mind. The thought made me want to burst out in tears. I forced myself to believe there was no way I was pregnant.

I brushed the idea off as I headed to the hotel room, changed clothes, and hurried back to the elevator and back downstairs. My parents and Justin waited for me in the lobby. We only had a few more hours in LA and we wanted to spend them shopping and eating. As we jumped into the car, my phone rang.

"Hi, Shaun," I said, picking it up. "How are you?"

"Congrats! Your dad told me what happened."

"Thanks. I'm so excited. But I wanted it to be a secret for a while."

"What's going on?" he asked.

"We're about to do a little shopping and grab a bite to eat. I'm sorry, I meant to have Justin call you when we got here, but he was asleep. Anyway, here he is."

I handed the phone to Justin, and they talked for a minute, afterwards we got out of the car to walk down Rodeo Drive. After two hours of shopping we were exhausted.

"I'm hungry and I want seafood!" my mom said. We walked back to the car while calling to make reservations at Stevie's for lunch. We sat down and took a moment to place our orders. So many thoughts raced through my head.

"I want to say something, but I don't want you guys to take it the wrong way." I said as our drink orders arrived. "I know I shouldn't question what God has planned for me," I said, "but I'm just trying to understand the timing. LombardiJones is set to open in a few days, it's all great but at the same time I don't want a lot on my plate."

For the first time ever my dad said not a word. He just kind of shrugged his shoulders.

"I've worked my whole life to make things easy for all of us. I'm almost there and at this point I just want to live and enjoy what I've done."

"I don't know how your feeling. But I will say never ask God for something and expect it to be easy. Life is a fight sustaining in it is also one. You can't be willing to bypass blessings you never thought would come to pass because you don't remember how you planted the seed. You either do it or you don't."

I had no response. We ate our meals in silence. After we finished we went back to the hotel to get ready for our flight.

We took a little longer than we'd expected to make it to the airport in just enough time to board our flight. Justin spent the seven hours on the plane coloring and snacking; my parents slept; and I daydreamed Tears ran down my face as memories of Grams ran throughout my mind.

We landed at John F. Kennedy Airport. My parents insisted on a driver, since they lived in the opposite direction of where I was going. I didn't mind giving them a ride but I gave in and they got into their car with their driver while Justin and I walked to my car in the airport's parking deck. I took Justin home; there was no traffic so it took me only twenty minutes. When I pulled up Shaun stood in the driveway. He opened Justin's door, and they embraced each other. I popped open the trunk for Shaun to pull out Justin's suitcase.

"Hey, Dila," Shaun said with a smile.

"Glad you're feeling better," I replied, smiling too.

"I cooked dinner. Would you like to join us?"

"Well, if you insist but let me do the dishes."

Walking into the house where we had once lived together, I got chills. It looked like a different place. But I tried not to focus too much on the changes.

"So where is this wonderful meal you speak of?" I asked, sitting down at the dining room table, spying some Chinese takeout boxes on the kitchen counter.

Shaun laughed. "Reheating it right now a day's that's what you women call cooking these days."

"Some women. Not all women. I actually cook, not reheat."

He smiled pouring the food into nice plates.

"Why even bother pouring them onto something you have to wash?" I asked. "Keep the food in the boxes it's in. It's okay with me." I reached for one of them.

"If you say so," He said handing me a fork. "I wanted to make it look pretty, just like women do."

I laughed again. "Presentation is everything."

Justin quickly eat his food not once coming up for air.

"Slow down," Shaun told him. "You're eating like you have not eaten all day."

"So how was the trip?"

"It was awesome!" Justin replied before I could. "We went shopping, we saw the Hollywood sign, we ate…' Justin again interrupted.

"Okay, I'm finished. Can I be excused?" he asked.

"Yes, you may." Shaun took his carton and put it in the trash. As Justin rushed off to his room, Shaun and I ate in complete silence.

"Thank you, Phadila," he said. "I swear, you're great. I'm sure you know that though."

I got up to throw away the empty take out containers.

"I know you may be tired of hearing it," he went on, following me in, "but I'm not tired of saying it. I really want another chance." He stated, waiting for my reply. I took a sip of my juice to make the moment a little less awkward. He clearly didn't mind.

"I don't know what to say. I'm just tired of you bringing it up."

"You don't have to say anything. I keep bringing it up because I want to make sure you understand where I stand. I'm willing to go to counseling. I'm willing to do whatever it will take to show you I'm for real this time."

I yawned, trying to signal that I was tired. Shaun gazed in silence. "Well maybe I'll think about it. Therapy doesn't sound like a bad idea."

"Cool. I'll have my assistant set it up."

"No!" I said. "I don't want anyone knowing anything until I know for sure that I'm willing to give you a second chance. I mean, I am. I just want to go slow, very slow!"

"Okay, okay. I'll take care of it myself tomorrow morning."

He smiled, I smiled back, but I headed for the door. "I'm tired. It's been a long day." He handed me my keys and kissed me on the cheek.

"We're going to be good. I promise." He opened the door walking me to my car. "Thank you," I said.

Chapter 25

I must have been extremely tired because when my alarm clock gave me a panic attack. It was another Monday. I couldn't believe it was finally happening Lombardijones would be opening its doors. I rolled out of the bed anxious hurrying to get ready and get to the office. I only had forty-five minutes to get to the ribbon-cutting ceremony, so I quickly showered, got dressed, and grabbed a bagel on my way out the door. I arrived at the office at exactly 7:50 a.m.

Friends, family, new employees, and several of our clients were waiting. I parked my car and made my way through the small crowd.

"Phadila!" my mom yelled. "I thought you were going to miss your own opening."

"I wouldn't miss this for the world." I stepped up in front and raised my voice to get everyone's attention. "I just want to speak really quickly. I would like to say thank you all for being here. My parents, family, and friends who have all helped me get company off the ground finally. This is a huge deal for me." I was ready handing the mic back to the Mayor.

My parents and I stepped up to the big, yellow band across the front doors of the building. We cut it together. We took a couple of pictures, did a little chatter, and went inside to begin our first day of work. I walked around handing out pieces of cake to everyone who wanted one, reintroducing myself, Mr. Johnson, the CEO of one of the local shelters that I hired a few people from, also walked around. Everyone is working together great," Mr. Johnson stated.

"Thank you. I would have to agree so far so good."

I felt like a million bucks.

I called a quick meeting as five o' clock approached with everyone in the office. "Hi, everyone." The room filled with whispers. "I don't want to take up too much of anyone's time but I would like to say thank you to all of you again. It means so much." I said, continuing. "Lombardijones is finally in business!"

Cheers roared around the room. I waited for everyone to get silent before I continued.

"If anyone wants to hang out for a while or if you want to take some pizza home to your kids, I bought plenty." Everyone stayed a little longer.

"This is so cool, Phadila. I appreciate you allowing me to be a part of all of this. You did it!" Sheena said, nibbling on a slice of cheese pizza.

"Girl, thanks! I didn't do it alone. This is partially your doing too. You have been a huge help and inspiration," I said, wrapping my arm around her neck for a hug.

"Girl, please!" She laughed. "This is all you. This is your moment. I am really proud of you."

I smiled. "Thanks, Sheena, that means a lot."

We hugged and watched as everyone enjoyed each other's company. We began to mingle with everyone in the room. I left that day on cloud nine. The biggest day of my life had finally come to pass.

*　*　*

After a couple months I could say we were officially doing well. But it was a lot of work. I sat in my office one rainy day going over contracts and thinking about how hard it had been to balance everything, not to mention going to therapy sessions with Shaun. We weren't officially together, but were doing very well. Honestly I appreciate the sessions because there is so much I didn't realize I needed to get off my chest.

As I continued to read through the contracts, there was a knock at the door.

"Phadila, there's someone here to see you." Sheena peeked her head into my office. I got up from behind my desk to greet whoever it was.

"Hello, how are you doing?" I said in complete shock. It was my old manager, Bill.

"Have a seat," I said. "Bill is everything going okay?"

"Everything is good business -wise. I came here to talk to you about something else."

Sheena had a confused expression on her face as she walked back in to offer him something to drink.

"Oh, no thank you," he said, waving his hand for her to leave the room. Sheena jumped at him from behind as if she were going to hit him. I smiled entertained.

"What's going on, Bill?" I asked as Sheena walked out. "What can I help you with?"

"Well, I found out that I'm battling cancer and according to my doctors I don't have long to live. I have no living family and I know that you are an extremely hard worker. You're dedicated, and you're one of the most ambitious people I have ever met."

I smiled. "Thank you."

"Well, what I'm trying to say is, I now own Wright & Wright. I would love for you to take over the company for me."

My mouth hit the floor. I didn't know what to say.

"It hurt me when you left," he went on, "because I saw a lot of myself in you. I know it's a bit much for you right now, and I can give you some time to think about it, but I don't think anyone could run the company better than you. I have already begun the process of stepping down. All I need is your signature and you would get everything."

Bill's company was one of the top business law firms in the state of New York. I had never expected to own it —especially not alongside my own company.

"I'm so sorry to hear that Bill," I said. "But I'll need some time to think about it. Wright & Wright is amazing company and it needs someone who can dedicate the time."

I sat my cup on the desk and noticing Sheena standing inside the door listening, nodding her head for me to accept Bill's offer.

"Bill, I'm so grateful you see me fit to carry on a huge legacy, but I have so much on my plate right now. I would definitely need to think this over." I smiled nervously.

"I understand. Please let me know. Otherwise I don't know whose hands the company will fall into."

* * *

Later that afternoon I pulled up outside the therapist's office and ran inside. I was five minutes late.

"Phadila, thank you for joining us," Therapist King said as I entered noticing that Shaun had already made it. I took a seat next to him.

"Phadila, we were talking about where things went wrong with you and Shaun," Mrs. King informed me. "Shaun was saying it was when he started his music career."

I glanced at him. "Well, actually, it started before that. It happened gradually, and I kind of blew it off. It got worse probably a year or two after he got signed. He started bringing the things he did when I wasn't around into our home."

"That makes a lot of sense. Did you two address these issues when they first happened?"

"Yes and no," I went on. "I tried to, but he would always give me an excuse. Eventually I got tired of arguing. He always made it seem like I was nagging. I just wanted him to step up like I knew he could." I looked at Shaun but couldn't read his expression.

"Phadila, when issues arise especially when you're being disrespected you need to address how you feel about it so you can nip it in the bud. If you continue to let things slide, the other person sometimes naturally assumes what they are doing to you is okay because you haven't spoken up against it. Always remember you teach people how to love you, and communication is the most important way to do that."

"You're right. I guess I always looked to my parents as my source of how a relationship should be. I attempted to make him be what I wanted; never really caring what he wanted because I had this fantasy in my head that our relationship was going to be like my parents. So when we reached the point in our relationship where he seemed to not want to be there it hurt me a lot. "

"That's understandable. That's the problem with most relationships. One person wants it to be a certain way because it's what they know. However, you have to understand that every relationship is different, and what works for your parents may not always work for you."

Mrs. King was right. "I don't think you tried to change me in any way," Shaun said. "I just think there were moments when you were trying to make me step up to the plate when I really wasn't ready to."

"Going to counseling was a great idea," I said. "I'm glad we decided to do this.

"I'm glad too." He smiled as we headed to our cars. "What are you about to do? You want to get some ice cream for old time's sake?"

"Oh yeah, I can definitely go for something sweet."

We headed to the nearest Cold Stone Creamery, three blocks away. We ordered two vanilla ice cream cones, one with brownies and the other with Oreo cookies.

"It's nice to know we both need some help in some areas. Hopefully it will teach us different ways to find trust."

"Do you think you'll ever trust me enough to give me another chance?" Shaun asked as he walked me to my car.

"I don't know. Honestly, I miss having you around. I spent so much of my life with you. At the same time, a lot of things got out of hand,

and I just can't see putting myself through all of that again. We'll see."

I wasn't sure if giving Shaun another chance was a good idea.

"That's understandable," Shaun said. "I've never been the best candidate for relationships."

"I'm sure you're not the only one."

"Again, I apologize."

"Once is enough, Shaun, I get it!" All the constant apologies get a bit irritating.

"I will as soon as you change your mind," we both laughed at his response.

"It's late," he went on. "We should head out." He opened my car door.

"Thanks," I said as I got in.

Chapter 26

I got straight to work on making changes to several contracts for possible clients when I made it home. Later I took a shower and relaxed on my living room floor. I pulled out the envelope Bill had given me. I read every word and felt a little overwhelmed. I spent all night debating whether or not this was a good idea. Yes, I wanted the money for my family. But at the same time I'm learning, money isn't everything. I decided to give it a rest and get back to working on the contracts.

I woke up the next morning around nine, still lying on the floor. I had a doctor's appointment at nine thirty. I quickly grabbed my papers and rushed out the door. I raced down the highway running into the office out of breath.

"Ms. Lombardijones, how are you today?" Dr. Swartz asked as he came into the exam room closing the door behind him.

"I'm good, thank you for asking."

"So, what's going on today?"

"Well, something is not right with my body. I can just feel it."

"Okay, let's do the basics first." He listened to my heart and checked my blood pressure. He ran down every question he could think of. Lastly he gave me a cup for a Urine sample.

"Doctor Swartz, I need to get to work. Is it possible that you could call me and give me any updates?" I asked. "Yes," he replied. Afterwards I went to work, but it was hard to concentrate.

After two hours Sheena buzzed me. "Bill's on the phone."

"Thank you," I said, picking up the phone. "Hi, Bill. How are you doing today?"

Bill rambled on for several minutes, we finally got on the subject of the contract.

"I looked over everything," I said, "and honestly, I'm not sure I would be the best choice. I have so much on my plate right now, I wouldn't be able to give Wright & Wright the focus it needs.

"Phadila? Are you sure?"

"I'm sorry Bill but Yes! I cannot accept the offer. I'm sorry. "

"Phadila, you know I trust your judgment. So I'm going to say okay."

Before I could hang up the phone, Sheena was in my office.

"Phadila, have you lost your mind?" she asked. She had been listening in on the phone conversation.

"Sheena, you should not be listening to my calls." I said sternly.

"Oh, I wasn't. I was standing right outside the door." She smiled. "But are you serious? You're not going to accept his offer!"

"You deserve it and you will do a good job." She insisted. "How can we be so sure? I want to focus on my own company."

I nicely pushed Sheena out of my office and closed the door behind her. I sat on the edge of my desk, looking out the window at my old neighborhood. As I dazed out across the city skyline, Sheena walked back into my office.

"Phadila just think of all the money you will have," she said. I looked at her, smiled, and replied, "Money isn't everything Sheena. I have been working hard to build my own foundation." The room was silent for a few seconds until the phone rang again. I answered.

"Hello? This is Phadila Oh, hi, Dr. Swartz. How are you?" "Is everything okay?" Sheena whispered. I fanned her away and sat down. " Are you sure?"

The doctor had given me some news I was not ready to digest.

"Are you still there?" he asked several times.

"Yes," I replied. "Well, okay, Doc. Thank you again."

I hung up the phone Sheena was all in my face.

"What's wrong?" she asked.

I laid my head on the desk. "I'm pregnant," I told her. I could feel her expression without looking up.

"You're what?" she asked. "By who? Let me find out you been gettin' some cookie and ain't told nobody. Well, congrats, mommy to be."

I kept my head down. I couldn't figure out what I was going to do.

"Sheena, you can't tell anyone." I looked up at her. "I'm pregnant by Shaun."

"Oh my goodness! How long has this been going on? Girl, why have you kept me out of the loop? Dila, I tell you everything. But everything with you is a secret."

She went on and on, and I suddenly got the urge to cry.

"Oh, no," she wailed. "What did I say? What did I do? Honey, I know you're not crying over Shaun. Is he that bad? Did he give you something too? Like a disease? Why are you crying?" Sheena knew how to ask the right question "Because it was a one night stand months ago, I was drinking and he came over. I meant to get the morning after pill, but so much was going on I forgot it." My head fell to the desk again.

"Dila, you are so full of it, honey. You're never too busy to go to the pharmacy for a pill. Especially if you know you don't want any child. They have a drive through that's open twenty-four hours. Honey, you want this baby. I don't know why you're frontin' because you want Shaun back too. Everybody knows. We can tell by the way you look at him. Girl, please. This is Sheena you're talking to. I'm not just your assistant but your friend. I see right through all that. Tell him you're pregnant, have his baby, and get married. You are freaking yourself out right now for no reason."

I looked at her. "For real? You think deep down inside I want a baby right now?"

"Yes. Dila, you still love him. It's okay. We won't hold that against you. You know why? We all want you guys back together. And he already told us you guys slept together."

"What? When did he tell you guys that?" I asked.

"He told us because we kept asking him why he was trying to avoid seeing you. I guess he didn't want you to feel uncomfortable."

I looked out into space as she opened the door.

"Where are you going?" I asked.

"To get my camera to take a picture of your pathetic face,"

She laughed again closing the door behind her. I put my head back down on my desk.

Just when everything seemed to be working itself into existence, so were other things.

Chapter 27

I made plans to meet Shaun and Justin at the park after school. After finding out the new that I was pregnant I was nervous to even go.

As the rest of the day went on I didn't know if I was making myself feel sicker by worrying or if I was actually feeling sick. What I did know was I wasn't ready to spill the beans. I sat at my desk daydreaming, trying to come up with an excuse not to show up to meet Shaun and Justin. Just as I built up the balls to start dialing Shaun's number, he sent me a text message.

"Are we still on?"

I wanted to say no, but I couldn't. I replied, "Yes, see you soon."

I slowly got myself ready and walked even slower to my car. I drove to Prospect Park as slow as I could without the New York City drivers cursing me out. The whole way I couldn't stop thinking about the abortion. I always wanted kids, but that moment alone tarnished my outlook on the possibility. It was hard to deal with, and I wasn't sure how Shaun was going to take it. I hoped he took it well. I saw him and Justin playing football in the distance and prayed I would go unnoticed until I got my mind together. The closer I got, the weaker and weaker I grew. I didn't understand why telling him would be so hard.

"Phadila, pull yourself together," I said to myself. "You've dealt with bigger issues than this."

"Mommy!" Justin spotted me. I waved and walked a little quicker so my mood would not be noticed.

"Hi, guys." I gave them both hugs and we sat down on a quilt to eat. I was afraid to look Shaun in the face, and he noticed.

"Is everything okay?" he asked.

I looked up. "Yeah well not really. I need to tell you something." He waited calmly and took a bite of his sandwich. "I found out that I'm pregnant."

He almost choked. "Oh, wow!"

"Congratulations!"

He laughed and shrugged his shoulders. "That's cool."

"What do you mean *that's cool*?"

"I mean I'm happy. We're having a baby. I've always wanted a little girl."

I smiled, happy that I wouldn't end up in the abortion clinic again. He leaned over and ran his hand over my ponytail.

"I know you're worried about all the what ifs," he said, "but we'll be good. I promise."

I knew he was serious from the way he looked at me. That made me a little more relaxed.

"Things will work out as they should, Dila." He kissed my lips softly.

"Now wait. Who said I'm giving you another chance?" I asked.

"No one. But I'm sure you will eventually. I'm wearing you down and you know it." We both laughed.

"You're so silly, but I'm feeling all kind of ways because I still think about the abortion I had previously." I replied. Shaun quickly pulled the straw of his juice box out of his mouth. "We were pregnant before?" He asked.

"Oh no! I was pregnant by Chris. I was so stuck on stupid I didn't want him to leave me that I let him talk me into going through with it." Tears began to form in my eyes. "Phadila, one thing I never understood about you was that; you are so focused and strong willed in every other aspect of your life. Yet when it came to men you always fell short somewhere." Shaun stated.

"Wow, really Shaun? Is that what you think of me?" I replied upset. "No, no... I just don't understand." Shaun made an effort to amend his previous statement. "Well Shaun, not everyone is strong in every aspect of their lives. But I've learned how to carry the days." I continued, "When you and I didn't work out I was extremely hurt because I had invested so much into our relationship. I thought I had it all figured out, especially after therapy." Shaun adjusted himself then replied, "Phadila one thing you must always understand is you are not your parents. You don't know every detail of their relationship enough to know what they went through to be the strong unit they appear to be now." Shaun was every bit of right. "I know that now, but I had to go through some things before I realized it for myself. Its life, some of us don't wake up knowing everything." I replied sarcastically, "Don't get cute, I don't know everything. Never will." Shaun responded.

"I've always known that you would end up with me, even when I called myself being tough." I replied. "Phadila, everyone knew that. I mean you hadn't had many boyfriends you were waiting for me." He replied cocky. "Shut up! I may not have had many boyfriends but I've had several boys." I replied smirking sarcastically, implying my sexual history after Shaun. "Many? As in how many?" he replied curious. "That's none of your business, now is it?" I replied giggling as he leaned over to hug and kiss me in efforts to get me to tell...

Chapter 28

"Phadila, are you okay?" an associate asked after an early morning meeting.

"I'm good, just a bit drained and need to kick my feet up." I tried to downplay the fact that I was now about nine months pregnant and I was an emotional wreck. It didn't help that every free moment I was thinking about my previous abortion nor did it help that Shaun was on the road.

"Are you sure? Let me get you some water." She walked over to the other side of the office to grab a bottle.

"Thanks," I replied with my head down. "I didn't know having a baby took you through every possible emotional thought or feeling in a matter of minutes."

She laughed. "Yeah, it's part of the process. You'll be okay." she began to gather her things. "Well, I have to go, but I hope you feel better. I'll tell everyone to keep an eye on you while you're in the office."

I sat at my desk, barely managing to take notes on a new client's case. My phone rang, giving me another distraction from actually working.

"Hello… This is she." It was Justin's teacher. "He did what? My son Justin? Are you sure?"

As she explained what had taken place, I lost more and more energy. "I'll be right there to pick him up." I hung up the phone. I could not believe Justin had gotten into a fight at school.

"This is not what I need right now!" I said, stacking the papers on my desk. I was tired therefore had no plans to come back to finish anything that I had spent most of the day not attempting to finish. Once I walk out the door I was done for the day.

I waited patiently for the elevator. I headed to my car and starting to feel even sicker than before. I took a sip of the water my employee had given me but that didn't help.

I pulled up at the school, the school's principal met me in the hallway.

"Hi, Ms. Lombardijones," he said.

"Hi, how are you?" I replied. We walked to his office, where Justin, his teacher, and another student and his parent sat waiting.

"Ma'am," the principal began, "we called you because Justin and one of his classmates got into a fight over a pencil. Apparently, in the midst of the fight, some words were said."

I looked over at Justin, who held his head down in shame. He already knew what time it was. I don't like coming to the school for unnecessary things.

"What were those words?" I asked, starting to feel light-headed.

"The word was *stupid*."

I stop to think for a minute, to make sure I heard him clearly. "You suspended him for calling someone stupid? I left work early for my son calling someone *stupid*?"

I became so agitated. "You've got to be kidding me, maybe a warning, but suspension?" I stood up, grabbed my purse and motioned for Justin to get up too.

"Mom, he called me stupid first," he said in his defense.

"Grown folks are talking," I told him. "I'll deal with you afterward. So he's suspended and what else?" I asked the principal. He and the teacher seemed taken aback by my response.

"Well, just for the rest of today," the principal responded.

"Thank you." I signaled for Justin to get his stuff, and we left.

"I'm sorry, Mom, but he took my pencil and he called me stupid first," Justin said as we walked hand in hand.

"You and your dad can talk about it later because I'm not in the mood right now. You know better than to go up to that school full of white folks acting a fool over a dang on pencil. I don't care if he was bothering you first, you tell your teacher. You don't take it upon yourself to just do what you want." I continued rambling on about the incident as we sat in the car riding home, typical parent behavior.

The closer we got, the harder it became to fight my dizziness. I pulled into the garage and Justin rushed into the house. I sat there, the motor still running. I was hardly functioning.

Luckily my phone rang. It was Shaun checking in on me.

"You okay?" he asked.

"I'm good. Just feeling really light-headed, but I'm sure it's nothing."

"Are you sure? I can come home early if you need me to." He worried.

"No, I'm okay. I'll eat something and I should be fine."

I played it off, but something told me it would get worse before it got better.

"I'll let you rest. I just wanted to check in on you. I love you."

We said our goodbyes, I walked into the house laid all my items on the kitchen countertop.

"Justin! Are you hungry?" I yelled.

"Yes, can I just have two hot dogs please?" he yelled back. I ran the water to boil the dogs in. I grabbed a Capri Sun out of the refrigerator for him to drink and sat down in the living room to rest.

Two hours later I woke up in so much pain I could hardly move.

"Justin! Justin!" I yelled, almost in tears. He came running. I could tell I had frightened him.

"Call Grandpa," I said. "I need to get to a hospital."

I tried to pull myself up but couldn't. Something was wrong, and I had known it all day.

"Justin can you help me up?" I called he came back into the room. He struggled but it was no good. We waited until my dad showed up a short while later.

"Phadila! Are you okay?" Dad asked rushing down the hallway to my room.

"I need to go to the doctor ASAP. Something is wrong!" I said in tears.

"Okay. Justin, get your jacket and find Mommy's purse and keys." My dad helped me walk to the car.

"It hurts really bad!" I cried.

"Can you make it to the car? Otherwise we're going to have to call an ambulance."

We kept walking and I kept fighting through it. "I'm fine," I said. "I'm fine. Let's just get there. I feel like this baby is about to come out, like it's stuck between my legs."

When we pulled into the driveway of the emergency room, Dad got me a wheelchair and pushed me inside. "Is everything okay ma'am?" asked the lady inside of the hospital.

"I don't know. I haven't been feeling good all day, and I'm in pain." I explain as I was out of breath from the aching in my body.

"Let's get you into a room." She pushed my chair down the hallway rushing to get me settled into a room. I laid the for about an hour before my doctor arrived. A couple nurses came in to talk, but I understood none of what they were discussing; which didn't help to ease any of my worries.

"Ms. Lombardijones?" The doctor stood over me, tapping my shoulder.

"Yes, what's wrong?" I replied.

"The baby is ready to come out."

"What! No, no. Call Shaun! Can we wait until he gets here? Where's my dad?" I needed support. I couldn't possibly have this baby without them around.

"Your dad is in the waiting room, and Shaun is on the first plane out of DC. I've already spoken to them both. Some of your other family and friends are in the waiting room. But we don't have time to wait, Phadila. The baby is ready to come now!"

The doctor asked my mom to come into the delivery room to give me some support.

"We're going to give you some anesthetics so you won't feel much pain," a nurse said while placing a needle into my IV. I swear I pushed and pushed for almost five minutes before we started hearing crying. I had used so much of my strength to push I didn't have much to open my eyes to see my new baby girl. I laid in the bed for a few minutes tired, watching the nurse clean up my baby.

"Where's my baby?" I asked the nurse as she seemed to be wiping down some tools. The room was extremely quiet.

"She's fine, your husband and family are all looking at her through the window in the hallway. She's so beautiful," she replied. My heart jumped to my throat. I thought maybe something wasn't right.

"Hi, Doctor," I said as he walked through the door.

"Ms. Lombardijones, how are you feeling?" he asked, smiling.

"I feel okay. Those drugs helped a lot, but I'm sure they'll wear off soon."

He laughed replying, "She's a beautiful baby. Congrats!"

I began to cry. "My God, I want to see her" I laid my head in my hands. "Is my family still here?" I asked.
"Yes. I can tell them to come in if you'd like."

"Phadila?" Shaun's head peek around the door.

"Shaun!" I motioned for him to come in.

"I got here as soon as I could." He came over and grabbed my hands tightly. "I'm glad you and the baby are okay. Did you pick a name yet?"

As tears rolled down my cheeks I replied, "no I was waiting for you."

"I'm not sure of what to name her. I mean there are so many names. What about Shauna? Monica?"

"Whatever you want to name her is fine with me." I said. I didn't care I was happy it was all over.

"Shauna will do! She'll fit right into this family." I smiled happy.

Four Years Later

"Can you believe we've been in counseling this long and now we are finally done?" I said to Shaun who was driving us home from our monthly date night. "Though I was very unsure about how much it would help us it really has helped a lot." Shaun smiled pulling the car into the drive way of our new home.

"Yea Babe you're right. I suggested it but I really had no idea."

"Aww we're home, I missed my babies." I said continuing, "And I have an early morning tomorrow." I said pacing behind Shaun a few steps as he began to open the front door. He turned on the entry way from there all I heard was, "Surprise!"

Startled, I looked around to see what in the hell was going on. There stood our families, friends and our three Kids, Justin, Shauna and our one year old son Michal.

"Hi everybody" I replied confused. "Dila, I know you're a bit confused on what's happening but this isn't just one of our usual date nights. On this day today we were thirteen years old when I confessed to you that I had the biggest crush on you. Remember the cherry ring pop I bought you asking you to be my girlfriend?" I smiled because I remembered that day like it was yesterday. Shaun continued," Well, today I wanted to tell you that since we were kids I loved the way you looked at me when you said my name. I love your smile, your unwanted opinions, your amazing ability to know my true heart, and I love the way you love me and our children." As Shaun continued to speak I could read the anticipation in everyone's face and I couldn't take it any longer...

As I shouted! "Damn it Shaun, I've been waiting for this day too long! Just ask me already so that I can say YES!" Excited I put my left hand in his hand.

"Ask you what Phadila?" Shaun replied acting all confused. "You know what! Ask me already." Shaun looked at me as I looked at everyone around the room for reassurance that he was about to ask for my hand in marriage.

But, he didn't ask. "Babe, this isn't a proposal. I just wanted to do something nice for you tonight." Shaun replied. Everyone in the room shook their heads agreeing with him. "Ughhh! Well save the long speech, you could have given me a card or some shit. Let's just have a good time!!" I replied embarrassed and upset. It was time we got married I thought to myself.

I walked out of the living room, through the dining room and into the kitchen to pour myself a glass of red wine. I took a sip refilled my glass, took another sip refilled my glass, and then walked back out into the living room to find Shaun down on one knee with a card and a red ring pop.

"Yes! Yes! Yes!" I screamed not caring that I had wasted red wine on my carpet and myself. "Phadila Lombardijones I love you! Will you marry me?" He asked. So excited I jumped on him as he was still kneeling on the floor. As we tumbled over backwards I could not stop crying and kissing him. It had finally happened; I was finally going to be Mrs. Shaun Michal!

The Author

Yashica M. Smith was born in Seattle, Washington in the 1982, first daughter of Deborah Reece & the only child of Larry Charles Smith. After her birth Yashica's mother relocated back to Holcomb, Mississippi where Yashica's parents were originally from and where her younger sister Nikki Wright was born June 1986. After Yashica's mom and step-dad separated; Yashica, her mother and her sister relocated back to Seattle, where she and her sister were raised by their mother.

After graduating Franklin high school, Yashica courageously relocated to Atlanta, Georgia to attend the college she dreamed of since she was a kid; Clark Atlanta University. Yashica involved herself in promotions and marketing for various record labels, radio stations and magazines. She wrote for many different entertainment blogs and online magazines under the pen name AutumnJones. Yashica was extremely active in the community and Clark Atlanta's Student radio Station, WSTU 98.1FM. She graduated from Clark Atlanta University in 2006, with a B.A. in Mass Media Media Arts.

In 2009 Yashica was laid off from her job after receiving the highest financial raise for any employee that year, at wit ends with one of her roommates and facing the end of their lease that she finally made the decision that shifted her life. She relocated back to Mississippi where her mother now resided due to her grandma's illness and save up some money. In the process she also wrote three other manuscripts, created many pieces of artwork and put together a collection of poetry. March of 2010, she moved to San Francisco. Yashica's journey in San Francisco was what she needed spiritually and artistically. Her journey was short lived after Yashica lost her completed manuscript due to her computer breaking. Upset, hurt and broken she was then back to square one. Eventually deciding it was time to relocate back to Mississippi especially since both of her grandmother's were sick in their last days of their illnesses. September 2010, Yashica was back in Mississippi.

This time it was different, previous visits Yashica hated to be in Mississippi but she found the peace of mind she needed. In just three weeks Yashica had re-written her manuscript and after spending months of editing; Yashica was back at an emotional loss when a high school friend was killed in a car accident, followed by her grandmother Mrs. Nancy Wright passing a week later, her other Grandma Mrs. Tottie Mae Smith in April and her aunt Mrs. Betty Wright in May. Yashica was an emotional wreck internally but she pressed on. Yashica is now a single mother ready to embark on her life's purpose and would love for you to experience what is to come.

Made in the USA
Monee, IL
23 December 2022

23508191R00181